I AM SLAPPY'S EVIL TWIN

GOOSEBUMPS®

Also available as ebooks

NIGHT OF THE LIVING DUMMY
DEEP TROUBLE
MONSTER BLOOD
THE HAUNTED MASK
ONE DAY AT HORRORLAND
THE CURSE OF THE MUMMY'S TOMB
BE CAREFUL WHAT YOU WISH FOR
SAY CHEESE AND DIE!
THE HORROR AT CAMP JELLYJAM
HOW I GOT MY SHRUNKEN HEAD
THE WEREWOLF OF FEVER SWAMP
A NIGHT IN TERROR TOWER
WELCOME TO DEAD HOUSE
WELCOME TO CAMP NIGHTMARE
GHOST BEACH
THE SCARECROW WALKS AT MIDNIGHT
YOU CAN'T SCARE ME!
RETURN OF THE MUMMY
REVENGE OF THE LAWN GNOMES
PHANTOM OF THE AUDITORIUM
VAMPIRE BREATH
STAY OUT OF THE BASEMENT
A SHOCKER ON SHOCK STREET
LET'S GET INVISIBLE!
NIGHT OF THE LIVING DUMMY 2
NIGHT OF THE LIVING DUMMY 3
THE ABOMINABLE SNOWMAN OF PASADENA
THE BLOB THAT ATE EVERYONE
THE GHOST NEXT DOOR
THE HAUNTED CAR
ATTACK OF THE GRAVEYARD GHOULS
PLEASE DON'T FEED THE VAMPIRE

ALSO AVAILABLE:
IT CAME FROM OHIO!: MY LIFE AS A WRITER by R.L. Stine

I AM SLAPPY'S
EVIL TWIN

R.L. STINE

SCHOLASTIC INC.

Goosebumps book series created by Parachute Press, Inc.
Copyright © 2017 by Scholastic Inc.

ISBN 978-1-338-06839-9

10 9 8 7 6 5 4 3 2 1   17 18 19 20 21

Printed in the U.S.A. 40
First printing 2017

SLAPPY HERE, EVERYONE.

Welcome to My World.

Yes, it's *SlappyWorld*—you're only *screaming* in it! Hahaha.

Feeling lucky, slave? I'm lucky because I'm ME! Haha. I mean, what if I was YOU? I don't even want to *think* about it!

I'm so good-looking, the mirror *begs me not to leave* every time I gaze into it. Ha. The only reason I'm not on a postage stamp is because no one can *lick* me! Hahaha.

Know what's almost as awesome-looking as me?

I don't, either! Hahahaha.

I'm so awesome, I give myself *goosebumps*! Ha. And guess what? Today is your lucky day. Today you get *two* of me for the price of one.

Don't thank me till you've read my story. Of *course* it's a scary story. It's about a boy named Luke Harrison. Luke lives in Hollywood, and his father makes horror movies.

1

Poor Luke. Before the story is over, Luke is *living* in a horror movie! He's not only screaming for help—he's seeing *double*! That's because he has *two* living dummies in his house. Hahaha.

Guess what? I may not be a good houseguest—but I tell a good, creepy story.

I call this one *I Am Slappy's Evil Twin*!

It's just one more terrifying tale from *SlappyWorld*.

PROLOGUE
1920

Franz Mahar strokes his white beard and gazes down at the face of the puppet he is making. The glassy olive-green eyes stare up at him. The doll's wooden face is still unpainted. The smooth lips are frozen in a pale grin.

From the open window of his workshop, Mahar hears the bleating of sheep. The farmers of the small village herd their flocks to the high pasture every morning. Then they bring the animals down as the afternoon sun begins to lower itself over the sloping hills.

The village stands eighty miles from the nearest large town. Nothing has changed in a hundred years. Cows and goats and pigs roam free. Mahar awakes to the sound of clucking chickens every morning.

Mahar raises a long needle and leans over the worktable. He begins sewing cuffs on the puppet's stiff white shirt. His fingers tremble.

He is an old man now, with failing eyesight

and unsteady hands. Once he had been a star of the London stage. He had created a ventriloquist dummy so lifelike, audiences were amazed. They filled theaters to see his act. He had fame and enough money to enjoy it.

But then, there had been trouble. He shared the stage with the magician Kanduu. With his swirling scarlet cape and his ability to make *anything* appear or disappear, Kanduu was also a star.

They became friends. Mahar trusted Kanduu. He didn't realize—until too late—that Kanduu's magic came from a dark place. Kanduu was a sorcerer.

He could cast spells, and his spells were always evil. He could control people. He could make them say and do things they didn't want to do.

Mahar learned a lot of magic from Kanduu. He didn't realize that Kanduu had an evil side. Until one day backstage when Mahar was about to begin his act.

He opened the long black case in which he kept Mr. Wood, his dummy. He bent down and began to lift the dummy from the case.

"Oww!" Mahar cried out as the dummy's wooden hand swung up and punched him hard in the chin.

"Keep your hands off me!" Mr. Wood shouted. Mahar stood there, staring in shock at him, rubbing the pain from his jaw.

"I'm pulling the strings from now on!" the dummy declared. He swung his wooden fist again and caught Mahar on the shoulder.

Backing away, Mahar realized what had happened. Kanduu had enchanted the dummy. Kanduu had poured his evil magic into Mahar's creation. Mr. Wood was *alive.*

Terrified, Mahar slammed the case shut. He left it on the stage. He never wanted to see that dummy again. He packed a bag and sailed for the United States.

Mahar was desperate to flee, to leave the evil dummy behind. He hid away in this tiny farm village and built a small cottage and a workshop. He lived quietly, alone. He made no friends.

He *built* his only friends. The puppets and dolls he created in his workshop were works of art. His hands gently carved their wooden heads and hands. He painted their faces. He sewed their costumes.

He gave them personalities. He did puppet shows and ventriloquist acts for himself. And once in a while, he used the magic he had learned from Kanduu. Some nights, he brought his puppets and dummies to life. He did it out of loneliness. He needed someone to talk to.

So today—while the sheep bleat and the chickens cluck outside his window—Mahar puts the final touches on his latest creation.

He finishes coloring the dummy's cheeks with gentle strokes of a small brush.

"You are made from the finest hardwood," he tells the dummy. "And I have used the powers I learned to give you life."

On its back on the worktable, the dummy blinks its glassy eyes.

"You will obey me at all times," Mahar says, pulling it up to a sitting position. He ties the dummy's polished brown shoes.

"The magic I have poured into you can be dangerous. You must stay under my control. You must not follow any angry or cruel thoughts."

The dummy blinks again. Does it understand Mahar's words?

Mahar has more instructions for his creation. But he is interrupted by a knocking on the wooden cottage door.

He jumps in surprise. "Who is pounding on my door so violently?"

It sounds like more than one fist beating at the door, hard enough to break it open.

"I'm coming. I'm coming," Mahar murmurs. He sets the dummy onto its back on the worktable.

Then he wipes his aged hands on the sides of his overalls and limps to the door. He pulls it open slowly—and utters a loud gasp.

The entire village?

Mahar's eyes blur as he sweeps his gaze over

8

the grim-faced men and women. At least two dozen of them. His legs begin to tremble. He tries to focus. Some of them carry torches. The men standing at the front of the group carry pistols.

Mahar feels his throat tighten. He begins to choke.

Finally, he finds his voice. "What do you want? Why are you here? What are you going to do?"

2

They all begin to shout at once. They shake angry fists at him. The flames from the torches shoot forward, as if attacking him. Men raise their pistols high in warning.

"Please—" Mahar begs. "Please—"

Two farmers in overalls lower their shoulders and push Mahar back from the doorway. He stumbles against the wall. Shouting and cursing, the villagers burst into his cottage.

They fill his front room. They wave the flaming torches angrily. A flower vase crashes to the floor. In the roar of voices, Mahar struggles to hear their words.

"Please explain—" he begs.

The two farmers step up to him. They are big men, tall with big bellies behind their overalls. Mud clings to the cuffs of their pants. One is bald, the other has shaggy blond hair that falls around his face. Their red foreheads are dripping with sweat.

10

"I am Buster Bailey," the bald one declares. "My neighbor here is Seth Johnson. I believe you've seen us in the village."

Mahar nods.

They narrow their eyes at him. "You know what you have done," Bailey growls.

"N-no," Mahar stammers. "I . . . I have done nothing."

"It is you who has brought the bad luck to our village," the farmer says through clenched jaws.

"Yes, it is you," Johnson repeats, shaking a meaty fist. "Our village is in ruins. The crops have withered and died."

"But—but—" Mahar sputters.

Johnson raises his hand to silence him. "The cows are all giving sour milk."

"Yesterday, a two-headed goat was born on my farm," Bailey growls. "The evil spreads from day to day. And *you* are the one who has brought it to us."

His words make the crowd of villagers begin to shout out their anger. Mahar sees some of them raise fists. They move forward, ready to attack.

He tries to protest. But their shouts drown out his words.

"It's the dolls!" a woman cries. Her face is red and angry beneath a long gray scarf. "Look! There's a new one!"

They turn to the dummy on its back on the worktable.

"The doll! It's the doll!"

"Destroy it!"

"The doll is evil. Look at that evil face."

Bailey grabs Mahar by the front of his work shirt. "Your dolls have brought a dozen misfortunes to our village."

"N-no—" Mahar stammers. "No. You are wrong. They are just dolls, made of wood and cloth."

"Evil! Evil! Evil!" Some villagers begin the chant.

All eyes are on Mahar's dummy. The villagers' faces are twisted in fear.

"Evil! Kill the evil! Kill the evil!"

Bailey shoves Mahar aside and strides to the workbench.

"No!" Mahar screams. But he is helpless to stop them.

The farmer grabs the dummy by its waist and hoists it over his head.

The shouts stop suddenly. A hush falls over the cottage. The dummy's arms and legs hang limply from Bailey's meaty hand. Its head is tilted back. Its eyes gaze glassily to the ceiling.

"Please—" Mahar begs. "The doll is my life's work! It took years to make. I beg you—"

The farmer lowers his shoulder and shoves Mahar out of the way again. Mahar stumbles back against the worktable. The two farmers start toward the door. The crowd steps back to allow them room to leave.

"Burn it!" someone shouts.

"Burn the doll!" cries the woman in the gray scarf.

"Burn it! Burn it!"

The farmers lumber out of the cottage. Bailey still holds the dummy high over his head.

His heart pounding, Mahar watches from the doorway of his cottage as the villagers work together to build a bonfire. His whole body trembles, and he feels as if his heart may burst open.

The smell of their fear lingers in his cottage. He can't erase their angry faces from his mind. Such hatred and superstition. How could these people suspect an innocent doll of bringing bad luck to their village?

The villagers work in silence. They stack tree branches and sticks of kindling in a high pile on the dirt road across from Mahar's cottage.

They scatter dead, dry leaves at the bottom to make the fire catch quickly. It doesn't take long to build a tall mountain of wood.

In the distance, Mahar hears the sad bleating of goats in their pasture. He tries to picture the two-headed goat.

He is still picturing it as the torches are lowered to the woodpile. The flames catch quickly. Mahar holds his breath and watches the fire climb the mound of sticks and branches.

When the flames have reached the top, the fire crackles and snaps. The yellow-orange flames dance and leap about.

The villagers have formed a circle around the bonfire. Mahar watches their eager faces, lighted by the fire. Their eyes are wide with excitement. The only sound is the crackling of leaves and sticks.

Johnson, his long blond hair glowing from the fire, breaks the silence with a booming shout. *"Good-bye to evil!"*

"Good-bye to evil!" villagers shout.

"Good-bye to evil! Good-bye to evil!"

Mahar gasps as Bailey heaves the dummy into the flames. The fire surrounds the dummy. Its suit jacket and pants erupt in flames.

And then, as Mahar watches from the cottage doorway, the fire swallows the dummy. It disappears into the swirling flames as if being eaten in one gulp.

And from behind the dancing, darting flames, a *howl* of pain and horror rings out over the crowd of silent onlookers.

3

All eyes turn to the cottage as the scream bursts through the air. It is Mahar's scream. And now he stands there on trembling legs, mouth still open, throat aching from his piercing cry.

Bailey and Johnson turn from the blaze and come striding heavily up to Mahar. Bailey points an accusing finger. "You must stop your evil work."

"If you want to remain in the village . . ." Johnson adds. "If you want to remain *alive* . . . you will heed our warning. You will stop your evil work."

Mahar sighs and shakes his head sadly. He lowers his eyes to the ground. "My work is over," he murmurs. His shoulders tremble. His voice breaks. "You have destroyed my life's work."

The two farmers stare hard at him for a long moment. Mahar can see the anger and hatred in their eyes. He watches them turn and make their way back to the villagers and the still-crackling bonfire.

Mahar slams the cottage door shut. He leans against the door, waiting to catch his breath. He wipes the sweat from his beard.

"The fools," he murmurs. "The stupid fools."

He peers out the cottage window to make sure no one is near. Then he crosses the room to a door hidden in the back of his workshop. His hand trembles as he opens it and turns on the lamp. He raises his eyes to the two dummies resting side by side on a shelf against the back wall.

"Did they really think I'd give up my precious dummy so easily?" he says to them. The dummies stare lifelessly straight ahead. They are identical in every way. The only difference: one has olive-green eyes. The other's eyes are black.

Mahar chuckles. "The fools . . . Did they really think I had but one dummy?"

He reaches for the green-eyed dummy and lowers it from the shelf. He cradles it in his arms. "They'll never get you," Mahar tells the dummies. "My friends. My true friends."

"Fools!" the dummy cries in a high, tinny voice. *"Fools!"*

Then both dummies toss back their heads, open their mouths wide, and laugh. Mahar laughs along with them. Laughs till he has tears in his eyes. The three of them laugh long and hard, enjoying the good joke.

THIS YEAR

4

Hey, guys, I'm Luke Harrison. I'm the red-headed kid poking around in the tool chest in the garage, trying to figure out what a Phillips screwdriver looks like.

Yes, I'm twelve, and I probably should know more about tools by now. But I'm not the mechanical type. I mean, the most complicated thing I ever built was a snowman!

That's a joke. Actually, I've never built anything in my life—until we decided to build this drone for a school contest.

"Hurry up, Luke. I can't hold this forever."

That's my sister, Kelly, across the garage. She's holding two pieces of the frame together. Kelly isn't much help, either. Well . . . she's good at holding things. And she's good at telling us what we're doing wrong. So I guess that's helpful.

Luckily, our friend Jamal is a mechanical genius. No. Seriously. He's a genius at this stuff.

He was one of those kids who built an entire city as big as his living room out of LEGOs when he was still in diapers.

Jamal bought the "Make-Your-Own-Drone" kit we're using. And when he spread all the pieces out in our garage, he didn't like the instructions. So he threw them out. He said he could do it better, and we believed him.

The drone is going to be pretty big. Bigger than our power mower. And yes, it's going to fly. Dad bought a tall propane tank to fuel it up once it's built.

And I know it will be built as soon as I find the Phillips screwdriver. I rattled the stuff around in the tool chest, searching for it.

"It's the one with the yellow handle," Jamal called. "Right on top."

He could spot it from across the garage. I told you he's a genius.

I brought him the screwdriver. Kelly held the two pieces of aluminum together and Jamal fastened them, working the screwdriver easily, and tightening it until he couldn't turn it anymore.

"What's this piece?" I asked. I held up a narrow strip of aluminum. I waved it in Jamal's face. "This would make an awesome sword."

"That's one of the propellers," Jamal said. "We're not ready for that."

"Give Jamal some space," Kelly said, waving me away.

Kelly is two years younger than me, but she's very bossy. She's always telling me to back off and let Jamal work. She's the baby in the family, and she's cute and blond with dimples in her cheeks. So she thinks she's something special.

I don't mean to sound harsh. Kelly and I get along really well. Especially if I do whatever she says.

"Here's what has to happen," Jamal said. "We do it in the right order. First the frame. Then the propellers. Then the motors."

I set the propeller piece down beside the others. I turned and studied the motors that were lined up against the wall. The drone had four motors. We had special batteries for the motors. And then a small propane tank for the back of the frame. I guess for liftoff.

Kelly and Jamal began to assemble another side of the frame. The afternoon sun slid behind some trees, and shadows swept over the garage. I stepped to the back wall and clicked on the garage lights.

"Don't say I'm not helpful," I called to them. They ignored me.

I turned and stumbled over the big propane tank. The tank was huge, about three feet taller than me. It looked like the water heater we have in the basement.

I stumbled into it, and as I watched in horror, the tank began to tilt and fall over.

I made a wild grab for it. But it was too heavy. It slipped right out of my hands.

Like a nightmare, the whole thing seemed to be happening in slow motion. The tank was going down, about to crash onto the hard concrete garage floor.

I grabbed for it again. Missed.

And then I screamed. "Look out! It's going to BLOW!"

With a gasp, I lurched forward. I wrapped my arms around the tall metal tank. "Hunnnh." A groan escaped my throat as I held on . . . held the tank upright. And with a desperate tug, I managed to stand it up again.

My heart was pounding so hard, I could feel it in my chest. I turned and saw Kelly and Jamal staring at me. They hadn't moved. They were still on their knees on the garage floor, holding on to the drone frame.

"Luke—were you *joking*?" Kelly demanded.

"I wish," I muttered, wiping the sweat off my forehead.

Jamal narrowed his eyes at me. "You mean you almost turned this into a horror movie?"

I nodded.

We talk about horror movies a lot in my house because that's what my dad does for a living. Dad is owner of Horror House Films. He produces horror movies.

If you're into horror, maybe you've seen some of his films. *Attack of the 2,000-Pound Dachshund*? *The Creature from the Cincinnati Suburbs*? He's made at least a dozen of them.

Dad brings home a lot of the things he uses in his films—creepy masks and costumes and all kinds of skeletons and skulls and monster heads. He lets us borrow some of them. It's a lot of fun for Kelly and me. We put on horror plays in our basement with them.

Some of the stuff he brings home is valuable. He keeps those things in display cases up in the attic. He calls it his Horror Museum.

He's always telling us how lucky we are. He says, "How many houses up here in the Hollywood Hills have horror museums hidden inside them?"

The answer, of course, is *none*.

When I was little, I had nightmares about the scary things up in the attic. I dreamed that the skeletons and the monster figures came to life and were fighting above my head.

A few times, I woke up screaming. I really thought I heard the creatures thumping and bumping and growling above my bedroom ceiling.

Dad always calmed me down. "Monsters only come alive in movies," he would tell me. "Never in real life. Not once." And when I was nine or ten, the nightmares went away.

Still holding on to the propane tank, I gazed at

Kelly and Jamal. "You really are a jerk," Kelly said. She jumped to her feet. She likes to be standing up when she scolds me. That way, she can cross her arms in front of her and look angry, just like Mom. Mom lives in the Valley with her new husband. We stay with her every other weekend.

"Dad said not to go near the propane tank," Kelly said. "He said to stay away from it unless he's here with us."

Jamal nodded. "We don't want to be in a horror movie," he reminded us again.

Then a strange, shrill voice from the driveway called out: *"Well, kiddoes, you're in one NOW!"*

"Huh?" I turned to the open garage door—and gasped.

Kelly screamed. Jamal dropped the drone.

I stared in disbelief. Two identical ventriloquist dummies were standing there. Standing there and talking—all by themselves!

The dummies stood about three feet tall. They wore identical gray suits with red bow ties. Their shoes were black and shiny. Their eyes were wide, and they had ugly red grins painted on their faces.

"You—you—" I tried to speak, but I was so startled, no sound came out.

"You're in a world of horror now!" one of the dummies rasped. His voice was high and hoarse. *"Welcome to OUR world!"*

Jamal jumped to his feet. He squinted at the two dummies. "Who is out there?" he called. "Who is making them talk?"

"Who is pulling YOUR strings?" one of the dummies cried.

"WE'LL be asking the questions from now on!" his twin exclaimed.

Kelly backed away from the garage door. Jamal stood frozen, gaping at them in confusion.

I laughed. "Is that you, Dad?" I called. "Very funny. You scared us—for a second."

No reply.

The dummies grinned at us with their painted red lips. I saw that one had olive-green eyes, the other black. Otherwise, you couldn't tell them apart.

The green-eyed dummy took a step into the garage. He seemed to be walking without anyone controlling him.

"Dad?" I called. "Are you out there?"

"It's remote controlled," Jamal said, squinting hard at it. "Like those remote-controlled cars we had when we were kids."

"Like the drone we're building," Kelly said. "Dad must be controlling them from nearby."

"Your dad is toast!" the green-eyed dummy declared. He took another step toward us.

"Your dad is BUTTERED toast!" his twin added. His voice was hoarse and scratchy.

The green-eyed dummy swung around to him. *"That doesn't make any sense, dummy. Buttered toast? What's that supposed to mean?"*

"Don't pick on me. I thought it was funny. Why can't you ever be nice to me?"

"Because you're stupid, even for a dummy?"

I shook my head. "Dad," I shouted. "We're enjoying your comedy act. But it's getting lame."

No reply.

"Are you sure they're remote controlled?" Kelly asked Jamal.

He shrugged. "What else could they be?"

"Your new masters!" they both declared.

And then I heard a shout from the driveway. "Hey, kids? Kids? Are you in the garage?" It was Dad.

I snickered. "He's pretending he doesn't know where we are," I said.

The dummies collapsed in a heap. Their legs folded and they dropped to the garage floor. Their wooden heads smacked the concrete, bounced once, then lay still. They didn't move.

Dad appeared at the head of the driveway. He nodded to us, smiling. But his smile faded when he saw the two crumpled dummies on the ground.

Dad raised his eyes to me. "Hey, why'd you take the dummies from my car?"

"We didn't," I said. "We didn't bring them here."

Dad frowned at us. "Yeah, sure. I suppose they got up and walked on their own!"

A grin spread over Jamal's face. "Mr. Harrison, we know they're remote controlled."

My dad rubbed his beard with one hand. Dad has a short salt-and-pepper beard over most of his face. His black hair is swept straight back off his broad forehead. He has pale blue eyes that always seem to be studying you, like they're beaming right into you.

He's very slim, and he looks much younger than his age, forty. He dresses like a young person, too. He wears the same outfit every day—a black rock-and-roll band T-shirt over straight-legged jeans.

"Jamal, check out the dummies," Dad said. "They're not remote controlled. They're not robots or anything. They're just dummies."

Jamal walked over and picked one up. Its arms and legs hung limply. Its head tilted back. "It's heavier than I thought," Jamal said. He squeezed the dummy's middle. "No controls."

"But, Dad—" Kelly started.

"They walked into the garage," I said, "and they talked to us. You did their voices—right?"

Dad shook his head. "I wasn't out here. I was bringing groceries into the house." His blue eyes locked on me. "Oh. I get it—you're writing your own horror script. A new idea for one of your plays? Sounds like you're off to a good start."

"Dad, you've got to believe us," Kelly said. I could tell by her voice that she was upset—and a little frightened. "We're not making up a story."

Dad laughed. "Don't kid a kidder."

He took the dummy from Jamal. "I hope you kids have been practicing your screams of terror," he said.

Kelly opened her mouth wide and let out a shrill howl.

"Awesome," Dad said. "You're going to be a star!"

"I can't believe we're going to be in your new film, Mr. Harrison," Jamal said.

"I need a lot of extras for the crowd scenes," Dad replied. "You know. People to scream and run down the street in a panic." He lifted the other dummy onto his shoulder. "These two dudes are the stars, of course."

"What's the film called?" Kelly asked.

"*I Married a Dummy*. We tested the title and it got a ninety-eight-percent approval rating."

"Is that good?" I asked. I was making a joke, but Dad didn't get it.

He shoved one of the dummies into my arms. "Luke, help me carry this one up to the attic."

I took the dummy and swung it onto my shoulder. I began to follow Dad to the house. As I walked, the wooden hand bounced against my arm.

I stopped when I felt hard wooden fingers wrap around my wrist. "Whoa." The fingers tightened ... tightened ... tightened till they were digging into my skin.

"Dad!" I cried. "Dad—help. It's *hurting* me!"

Dad spun around.

"My hand—" I groaned.

He squinted at me. "What's wrong?"

The dummy's arm drooped limply now. The wooden hand hung lifelessly near the grass. Nowhere near my wrist.

"It—it grabbed my wrist," I stammered. The pain was still shooting down my arm.

Dad rolled his eyes. "Luke, give me a break. You can carry a joke too far, you know?"

"Dad, it's not a joke," I said. I held up my wrist. "Look. It's red."

"I don't see it," Dad replied. "Why are you doing this, Luke? If you don't want to be in the movie, just tell me." He rubbed his beard. "Are you really afraid of these two old puppets?"

"No. No way," I said. I could see that Dad wasn't going to believe me. So I shut up and followed him up the steep attic stairs to the horror museum. Kelly and Jamal trailed after us.

The attic is long and wide with a low ceiling and twin windows at both ends. Gray evening light washed down from the skylight above us.

The dark floorboards are old and loose. They creak and groan when you walk on them. Perfect for a horror museum.

Dad clicked on the ceiling lights, and the glass display cases all lit up. The cases are filled with shelf after shelf of treasures from old horror movies.

I glanced at the mummy hand from the original Mummy movie. Frankenstein's huge shoes from the first Frankenstein film. A shark jaw from the movie *Jaws*.

We walked along one wall covered with old movie posters. *The Creature from the Black Lagoon . . . Nightmare on Elm Street . . . The Brain That Wouldn't Die . . .*

Jamal hung back. I noticed that he kept his eyes straight forward. He didn't look at any of the displays or posters.

He never liked to come up here. He insisted he wasn't afraid. He said he just wasn't a big horror fan. "I like sci-fi movies better," he said. "The ones where they show all kinds of amazing bots, and virtual reality, and machines from the future."

Typical Jamal.

Dad led the way to an empty glass display case. He set his dummy down on top of it and took the other dummy from my arms.

I rubbed my wrist. It still ached. "Why are we locking them up in the attic if you need them for the movie?" I asked.

"They're very valuable," Dad said. "I need to keep them safe and sound."

"And when the movie is over?" I asked. "Are you going to keep them up here?"

Dad shook his head. "No. I'm going to sell them. I have two collectors who are dying to get their hands on them. One in Pasadena and one in Beijing, China. Do you believe that? Selling these dummies will pay for your college education."

"Wow," Kelly said. "They're *totally* valuable."

"You mean you're going to split them up?" Jamal asked, his eyes on the dummies. "Aren't they, like, brothers?"

"Yeah. They're identical twins," Kelly said.

Dad laughed. "Dummies can't be brothers. They're dummies. What's wrong with you kids? They're not alive. They only come to life in movies like the one I'm making."

We didn't say anything. I gazed at the two grinning dummies. I had a really bad feeling about them.

"Help me get them in the case," Dad said.

Kelly picked up one, and I picked up the other. Dad lifted the glass lid. We lowered the dummies into the case and set them down on their backs. Their glassy eyes stared straight up at the ceiling. We placed their arms at their sides.

Dad took a silvery key and carefully locked the case. He set the key down on a table across from us. "Don't play with them, okay?" he said. "Don't take them out of the case."

"That won't be a problem," I said, rubbing my wrist.

I've got to be honest. I like scary movies. In fact, I like all of my dad's movies. But these two grinning dummies were creeping me out. I was seriously glad they were locked in that case.

"How is the drone coming along?" Dad asked Jamal.

"Good," Jamal said. "The frame is almost built. We should be able to put on the propellers by the end of the weekend."

"Awesome," Dad said. "You'll need me to load the propane from the big tank into the drone."

"Maybe next weekend," Jamal said.

"That's excellent," Dad said. "I can't wait to fly it over the neighbors' houses and scare them to death." He laughed.

"You sure like to scare people, Dad," Kelly said.

His phone rang before he could reply. His ringtone is a woman screaming in horror. He glanced at the screen. "I have to take this," he said. He raised the phone to his ear and headed down the stairs.

I backed away from the glass case. "Those dummies were really talking, right? You heard them . . ." I said to Kelly.

"It was just Dad," Kelly said. "It had to be. He was playing a joke on us." She wandered along the aisle of display cases. "Have you seen these?" she asked Jamal. "Dad's new collection of vampire fangs. He has a little tag on each one to identify what movie it came from."

"Your dad is weird," Jamal said. "I mean, I like him. He's a nice guy. But he's weird." He shivered. "Can we go downstairs now?"

"Good idea," I said. I started toward the attic stairs.

But I stopped when I heard a sound.

Tap tap tap.

At first, I thought it was a bird at the window. We have a woodpecker who is trying to drill a hole in our house.

Tap tap tap.

I turned toward the sound. It was coming from the dummies' display case. I glimpsed Kelly's face. Her eyes were wide with shock.

I took a step toward the glass case. And

gasped when I saw one of the dummies, flat on his back, raise a wooden hand.

Tap tap tap.

He raised his hand and began to pound hard against the lid.

Tap tap tap . . .

Tap tap taptaptap.

"No!" I cried. "This isn't happening."

"He—he's trying to push his way out!" Jamal cried. He backed away, his face twisted in fear.

"This can't be," I murmured.

"Dad!" Kelly screamed. "Dad—come *quick!*"

No reply.

"He didn't hear us," I said. "He probably went into his office to take that call."

Taptaptap.

"Dad! Daaaaad!" she screamed.

No answer.

I held my breath as the other dummy raised both hands to the glass lid and began to pound. The two dummies were pushing the lid, knocking their wooden hands against it.

"Let's get *out* of here!" Jamal cried, his voice cracking in fright.

"No, wait—" I said. "Wait. I have an idea."

Taptaptaptap.

Jamal was halfway to the stairs. "Wh-what's your idea?" he stammered.

"We let them out," I said.

Kelly uttered a cry. Jamal made a choking sound.

"Are you *crazy*?" Kelly cried. "Let them out?"

I nodded. I pulled my phone from my jeans pocket. "Yes. We unlock the case and let them out. They'll climb out of the case and start talking to us the way they did in the garage."

I slapped my phone. "I'll get the whole thing on video. It will prove to Dad that we weren't lying. He'll *have* to believe us. He'll see that the dummies can walk and talk."

"No way!" Jamal cried, shaking his head. "No way, Luke. That's just crazy. And it's too dangerous."

"Jamal is right," Kelly said. "They're too frightening. We don't know what they'll do after we let them out."

"And how will we get them back in the case?" Jamal demanded.

"We need Dad," Kelly said, glancing to the stairway.

"We need Dad to *believe* us," I said. "He thinks we were joking. He thinks we made the whole thing up."

Tap tap taptaptap.

"I . . . I'm scared," Kelly said. "What if . . ." Her voice trailed off.

"I'm scared, too," I admitted. "That's why we have to get Dad to believe us. When he sees the video, he'll know we aren't lying."

"No. Please—I'm begging you," Jamal said. He backed into the stairway. "Please don't do it, Luke."

I looked from Kelly to Jamal. *Tap taptap tap. What should we do?*

I reached for the key . . .

SLAPPY HERE, EVERYONE.

Go ahead, Luke. Open the lid. What have you got to lose?

My brother and I won't do anything bad. I promise. And you can always count on a promise from an evil dummy—right? Hahahaha.

We just want to look around the attic. Maybe take a few souvenirs. Like your *heads*! Hahaha.

Think Luke will unlock the lid and let us out? Well, we'll see. But before we go back to the story, let me give you a little spelling lesson. The best way to spell *Luke* is L-O-S-E-R. Hahahaha!

I pushed the RECORD button on my phone and handed the phone to Kelly. She was so frightened, it almost slid through her cold, wet hand.

"Luke—don't." I heard Jamal's pleas from the stairway.

But I ignored him. I knew what I had to do. I turned the key in the lock and lifted the lid of the glass case.

"Huh?" We all gasped as the two dummies sprang up to a sitting position at once.

"Thanks for the fresh air!" the black-eyed one exclaimed. *"I was getting a leg cramp in there."*

"You certainly took your time!" the green-eyed dummy shouted. *"Now I'm going to take a LONNNNG time paying you back!"*

"Now, now, Slappy," his twin scolded. *"Don't frighten them. Why can't you ever be gentle?"*

"Snappy, why can't you ever be SMART? Is it because you've got sawdust for brains? Hahaha!"

"See?" the black-eyed one replied. *"That's why you have so much trouble making friends. You don't try to be nice."*

Kelly, Jamal, and I stood frozen, watching them argue, their wooden mouths snapping up and down, their eyes sliding from side to side. Kelly kept the phone raised, aimed at them, her hand trembling.

"D-dummies can't talk," Jamal murmured from the stairs.

The one named Slappy turned toward him angrily. *"Who you calling dummy, DUMMY?"*

"Don't call names," his twin scolded.

"SHUT UP, SNAPPY!" Slappy screamed. He lowered both hands to the side of the display case. Then he pushed up and flung himself out of the case. His shoes landed with a loud *thud* on the floor.

Jamal uttered a frightened cry. Kelly took a step back but continued to video him.

"Don't be so scared, kids," Slappy rasped. *"We're not frightening—we're only TERRIFYING! Hahaha!"*

"Don't be so harsh, Slappy," his twin said.

A growl escaped Slappy's open mouth. He turned and tugged Snappy out of the box. He slammed him hard onto his feet on the floor.

Then he turned back to us. *"My name is Slappy,"* he said, taking a small bow. *"My genius* brother is Snappy. *But from now on, you can call us MASTER! Hahaha!"*

"Be nice, Slappy," Snappy said quietly. His voice was softer than his twin's. He appeared almost shy.

Slappy ignored him. *"Your father thinks he can split us up. I heard what he said. But the only thing that will be split is his HEAD! Hahahaha!"*

His laugh was more frightening than his words. It was cold and cruel and didn't sound like laughter at all.

"No violence, brother," Snappy said, shaking his head. *"You know I HATE violence."*

I realized my heart was beating like crazy. My whole body felt cold and shaky. I glanced back at Jamal. He had his hands raised in front of him, like a shield.

"We're going to teach your father a lesson," Slappy rasped in his hoarse, shrill voice. *"We're going to make him PAY for thinking he can split us up. And guess what, slaves—you're going to HELP us! Hahaha!"*

"Don't force them, Slappy," Snappy said. *"That's no way to make friends."*

Kelly turned to me, raising the phone. "I think I've got enough, Luke. This video will definitely convince Dad."

I nodded toward the attic stairs. "Go. Fast. Show it to him."

She turned to go. But Slappy moved quickly. He jumped in front of her. He grabbed the phone from her hand. I heard a loud *cracccck* as he closed his wooden fingers around it.

"Hey—" Kelly made a wild grab for the phone. Missed.

Slappy skipped out of her reach, laughing.

"Give it back, Slappy," his twin said. *"You know that doesn't belong to you. Why can't you be considerate of other people's property?"*

Slappy's eyes spun, and he tossed both arms up and screamed in a rage. *"SHUT UP, SNAPPY! I'm warning you. Don't cramp my style, you blockhead!"*

"Names can never hurt me," Snappy replied in a singsong voice.

"Then how about this?" Slappy screamed. He swung his fist hard. It landed with a *thud* against Snappy's chest.

"No fighting! No fighting!" Snappy cried.

I watched, frozen in shock, unable to believe what I was seeing. Slappy attacked Snappy again. They punched each other, their wooden fists landing against their soft middles.

Screaming and calling each other names, they wrapped their arms around each other and pulled themselves down to the floor.

I jumped out of the way as they wrestled, rolling down the aisle. They punched and head-butted and kicked and bit each other.

"You're *MEAN*, Slappy. You've always been so mean to me!"

"You idiot! Snappy, you'll be a dummy for the rest of your life!"

Jamal was still frozen at the stairs. Kelly leaped out of the way as the dummies wrestled and rolled down the aisle.

I saw where they were heading. "Look OUT!" I screamed.

Too late. They barreled full-force into Dad's tall china statue of Edgar Allan Poe.

"Noooooo!" I screamed again as they hit it hard. They rolled into the legs of the statue and sent it toppling to the floor. It landed with a deafening *crash*—and shattered into a thousand pieces.

Shards of china went flying across the floor. The dummies, arms wrapped around each other on the floor, stopped fighting.

And as I stared at the mess all around, my dad's precious china sculpture . . . I heard his voice calling from the bottom of the attic stairs: "What's going on up there? Did I hear a crash? Did I hear broken glass?"

Before anyone could answer, Dad came charging up the stairs.

10

Dad burst into the attic, eyes wide with alarm. "What's going on, guys?"

Kelly, Jamal, and I stood frozen in place.

Dad took several steps toward us. At first, he didn't notice the missing Poe sculpture. But then his shoes crunched over pieces of broken china. He glanced down and groaned.

He dropped to the floor and gathered up a few jagged pieces. "The Poe statue? Is that what this is?" He gazed up at me.

"Uh . . . well . . ." Suddenly, I couldn't remember any words.

"You broke the Poe statue?" Dad's voice was a lot higher than usual. He dropped the chunks of china to the floor and stood up.

Jamal was the first one to find his voice. "We didn't do it, Mr. Harrison."

Kelly nodded. "It's true."

"Then who did it?" Dad demanded. "Elves?"

46

"The dummies did it, Dad," I said. "I . . . I did a stupid thing. I let them out of the case. They started to fight and . . . well . . . they knocked over the statue."

Dad studied me for a long moment. Then he turned to the glass display case at the end of the aisle.

"Oh no," I murmured. I saw them. The two dummies. They were back in the case, flat on their backs.

"No!" Kelly cried, stepping up to the display case. "No. It's impossible!"

Dad shook his head. "What did I teach you two about taking responsibility for the things you do?"

"You—you've got to believe us, Dad," I stammered. I couldn't take my eyes off the two dummies, folded up in the case, staring blankly at the ceiling. "I let them out. One of them is called Slappy. He was angry because you plan to split them up. He said he wanted to make trouble for you—"

Dad raised a hand to signal silence. "You've got a good imagination, Luke. You should write all this down. It's the start of the screenplay you're obviously working on."

"But, Dad—"

"No, I'm impressed. Seriously. I'm impressed that you can make up a crazy story like that on the spot. You didn't even take a breath." He rubbed his beard, his eyes locked on mine. "You broke my Poe statue. And two seconds later, you've got a story to get you out of trouble. Amazing."

"He's telling the truth, Mr. Harrison," Jamal said.

Dad waved him away. "I know you're their friend, Jamal. But you don't have to lie for them."

He rested his hands on top of the case and gazed through the glass lid at the two lifeless dummies.

"Wait a minute!" Kelly cried. "I have proof, Dad. I can prove that we're telling the truth."

Dad turned to her. "Proof? Ha. *This* I want to see."

Kelly moved down the aisle of display cases, searching the floor for her phone. Finally she found it surrounded by chunks of broken china.

"I have the whole thing on video," she said, raising the phone to Dad. "When you see this, you'll know we're telling the truth. And you will want to apologize to us for not believing us."

Dad crossed his arms in front of him. "Okay. Show me."

Kelly raised the phone. I could see from across the room that the screen was totally cracked. She pushed the HOME button. The screen remained black. She pushed it again. Nothing happened.

She shook the phone—and the back fell off.

"It's totally wrecked." She sighed. "Slappy cracked it with his wooden hand. He . . . he ruined it."

Dad tapped his fingers on a glass case. "How did you *really* wreck your phone, Kelly?" he asked. "Did you drop it?"

Kelly lowered her eyes and didn't reply.

"I guess you *don't* have proof," Dad said.

Kelly's shoulders drooped.

"And I guess you kids think you're going to blame everything bad that happens around here on the dummies. Well . . . you'd better stop that right now."

"But, Dad—" I started.

He covered my mouth with his hand. "No more."

"Mmmmm mmmppp mmmmmp," I said.

"One more incident with the dummies," he said, "and I won't use you in the movie. I'm serious. You'll miss all the fun. Promise me this is the last time."

"Promise," I muttered. What else could I do? I really wanted to be in the movie. So did Kelly and Jamal. And I wanted Dad to believe us. I didn't want him to think we were lying or making stuff up.

But I had to make sure those dummies didn't try to hurt Dad. I had to make sure they stayed in the case.

I looked for the key to lock them in—and gasped.

The top of the key was poking out of Slappy's pocket in the front of his jacket.

"Dad, look!" I said.

"I"m not looking at anything." He shook his head. "I've seen enough. Come downstairs."

I sighed as I followed Dad to the stairs. As I started down, I turned back—and saw Slappy move in the glass case. He turned his head and winked at me. Then he raised one hand and waved bye-bye.

11

The dummies weren't going to give up. They didn't want Dad to split them up. I knew they would keep making trouble.

What were they going to do to him?

I didn't know. How could I know what a wooden-headed dummy was thinking? All I knew was that we had to convince Dad he was in trouble. Somehow, we had to prove to him that we were telling the truth.

That wasn't going to be easy.

At dinner, every time Kelly or I said the word *dummy*, Dad raised a finger to his mouth and made a zipping motion over his lips. The word was forbidden.

Kelly and I sat helplessly, nibbling at our macaroni and avocado salad. We didn't feel like eating. I had a heavy feeling in my stomach and my throat felt tight, making it hard to swallow.

We tried to talk to Dad about our drone-building and about school and stuff. But I knew we both had only one thing on our minds—those two dummies.

It took me a long time to fall asleep that night. The ceiling in my room is low, and the attic is right above my head. Our house is pretty old, and it's at the edge of the hilltop overlooking the Valley, so it kind of tilts.

Every creak and groan and squeak made me gasp and sit straight up in bed. Each time, I was sure I heard the two dummies moving around up there.

Yawning, I tried putting the pillow over my head to block out all sounds. Finally, after midnight, I drifted into a light sleep.

But a *thump* at my bedroom door made me sit up again, wide awake and alert. "Hey!" I cried.

My bedroom door began to slide open. Before I went to bed, I'd made sure the door had clicked shut. But someone had turned the knob. Someone was slowly pushing the door open.

"Oh no." In the gray light from the hall, I could see the outline of the dummy's head.

He took a step into my room and came into clear focus. The dummy, half-covered in shadow, grinning his frozen, ugly grin. His eyes glowed in the inky darkness.

"N-no!" I stammered. I sat up and hugged myself, trying to stop the chills that ran down my body.

The dummy took another silent step forward. And I could see a figure behind him. The other dummy. They both slid across the carpet, moving slowly—as if in slow motion—toward my bed. Grinning. Eyes glowing like hot, evil coals.

Their hands were raised straight out in front of them, as if they were sleepwalking. As if they were coming for me. Their shoes made no sound on my bedroom carpet.

And then I saw a third dummy in the half-open doorway. It slid into the room. Identical. It was identical to the first two. And it crept toward my bed in a straight line, arms raised stiffly in front of it.

And when the fourth dummy appeared in the room, the whispers began. They moved silently, like shadows, as if they had no bodies at all. Four sets of glowing eyes . . . four evil, frozen grins . . .

Whispering. The four of them whispering in unison. The most terrifying sound I'd ever heard in my life . . .

"I'm Slappy . . . I'm Snappy . . . I'm Slappy . . . I'm Snappy . . ."

The stiff wooden hands reached for me. Reached for my throat.

I opened my mouth wide and began to scream.

12

I knew it was a dream the moment I sat up.

I knew it had been a nightmare, but my whole body was shaking, and my teeth were chattering. I squinted into the gray darkness. No one there. No dummies creeping across the rug.

"A nightmare . . . A stupid nightmare," I murmured, my voice clogged with sleep.

But I knew the dummies were still in the house. Still able to talk. Still alive. Still angry at my dad.

That wasn't a dream. It was a different kind of nightmare. A *living* nightmare.

I hugged myself, forcing the shudders to stop. Outside my bedroom window, I heard a truck rumble past. And I heard a burst of wind rushing through the trees. It always gets windy up here in the hills.

I took long, slow breaths, waiting for my heart to stop pounding.

And then I heard another sound.

A *thump*. A *tap*. Outside my room.

I turned to the door. It was still shut. Still the way I'd left it.

I held my breath and listened.

Another *thud*. Footsteps.

Yes. Footsteps on the other side of my bedroom door. Slow, thudding footsteps inching toward my room.

The dummies were out there. I could hear them clearly.

They had climbed out of the display case, come down the attic stairs. And now they were in the hall, moving together . . . moving toward my room.

No. They can't do this, I thought. *I won't let them do this. I'm going to stop them and show them to Dad.*

I let my breath out in a whoosh. Ignoring the chills at the back of my neck, I leaped to my feet. My legs were trembling. But I stumbled to the door.

With a low cry, I swung the door open and burst out into the hall.

A dim yellow night-light at the floor provided a faint circle of light on the wall. And beyond it, halfway down the hall, I saw him. Saw the dummy, hidden in a deep shadow.

I took a running start. Let out a hoarse cry as I ran. Lowered my shoulder—and tackled him to the floor.

13

"Luke? What are you *doing*?"

I blinked. It took me a few seconds to realize I had tackled Kelly.

There we were, sprawled on the floor in our pajamas. I had landed on her back, and I was pushing her face into the carpet.

"Oh, wow," I murmured. I struggled to stand up. Then I reached down and helped pull my sister to her feet. "I thought—"

She tugged her pajama bottoms straight. "Luke—have you totally lost it? You couldn't see it was me?"

"How *could* I?" I cried. "It's dark and—and—"

She shook her head hard. Her blond hair was tangled about her face. "Ow. I think you broke my ribs."

I stared at her. "Well . . . what were you doing out here?"

"I thought I heard something," she replied.

"Something in the attic?"

56

She nodded. "I think they're moving around up there."

"Should we tell Dad?" I said.

Kelly rolled her eyes. "Did you forget what he said about one more incident? *No way* we tell Dad. You want to be in the movie, and so do I. Anyway, he won't believe us."

"So . . . what should we do?" I asked.

She raised a finger to her lips. We listened hard and gazed up at the ceiling. I didn't hear anything up there. Were the dummies awake? Were they still in the glass case? Were they somewhere else in the house?

"I . . . I can't *stand* this," I admitted to Kelly. "It's like having two *monsters* living in the house. Two evil creatures. And we're the only ones who know they're here."

Kelly brushed a strand of hair off her face. "The one named Snappy seems kind of nice."

"It doesn't matter!" I exclaimed. "He's a *living dummy*. And he's living in our house. And Dad thinks we're crazy or liars or something."

Kelly turned her gaze to the attic door. "Let's go up to the attic."

"Huh? Are you joking?"

"Luke, we have to prove to Dad that we're not liars. He *has* to know the truth about them."

I put my hands on my waist. "And how do we prove it to him? They already wrecked your phone."

"That little video camera—remember? Dad gave it to you for your birthday?" Kelly said. "The GoPro camera. Go get it."

I hurried to my room and grabbed the little camera. Kelly was being brave, and I had no choice. I had to be brave along with her.

Did I really want to go up to the attic in the middle of the night? Would I rather stick my head down an alligator's throat?

But I couldn't let Kelly be the brave one. And I couldn't let her go up there alone.

That's my only explanation for why I did it. And, of course, it was a decision I regretted as soon as we climbed the stairs and stepped into the dark museum of horrors.

I fumbled for the ceiling light switch. Before I managed to click on the light, I saw eyes staring at me from all around the long, narrow room. The eyes of Dad's creatures. Werewolf heads and monster masks. A life-sized vampire sculpture. Bat eyes, glowing scarlet even in the darkness.

Finally, I managed to turn on the light. It flickered overhead, and all the creatures came into focus. Still scary, even in the yellow light. All the creatures appeared to be watching us . . . watching us and waiting to pounce.

Of course, I was letting my imagination run away with me.

But wouldn't *you*?

If the two wooden dummies could come to life, couldn't the *other* creatures begin to move around, too? Couldn't they begin to walk and growl and talk and . . . attack?

The little camera almost slipped from my hand. I realized my hands were ice cold and wet with sweat. I gripped the GoPro tightly and held it close to my chest as I led the way down the aisle of display cases.

"Get ready," Kelly said. She walked close behind me, close enough to bump me as we made our way to the back of the attic. "Get the camera ready, Luke."

I obediently raised the camera. I took a deep, shuddering breath. We stepped up to the glass display case. We both stopped a few inches away and peered down through the glass lid.

Empty.

The case was empty.

"G-gone," I stammered. I turned to Kelly. But before I could say anything more, I felt a hand grab my shoulder. Hard fingers pressed painfully into my shoulder from behind.

Kelly and I both started to scream, high wails of terror that shook the attic walls.

14

My knees started to fold. I grabbed the top of the case to hold myself up. The hard fingers dug into my shoulder.

I spun around—and stared at the grinning dummy, his green eyes alive with excitement. His wooden hand held its grip on me, squeezing so tightly, I wanted to scream.

"Enough playtime, kiddies!" he rasped in his tinny, hoarse voice. *"Let's make a REAL horror film!"* He tossed back his head and laughed his cold, ugly laugh.

I tugged free and staggered back to the wall. I tried to rub the pain from my throbbing shoulder. "Slappy—" I choked out.

I saw Snappy, his twin, standing against the wall. *"Slappy, play nice,"* he scolded. *"Why can't you ever get along with others?"*

Slappy spun on his brother. *"Shut your wooden mouth. I'll pound your head like a woodpecker!"*

60

Snappy shook his head sadly but didn't reply.

Slappy lurched forward and swiped the little camera from my hand. He turned it on Kelly and me. *"Okay—scream. Let's hear you scream! Give it all you've got!"*

Kelly and I couldn't help it. We screamed. I hoped our cries might wake up Dad.

"Why are you doing this?" Kelly yelled at Slappy. "Why?"

He ignored her question. He just tossed back his head and laughed again. Then he shoved the camera into Kelly's hands.

"Okay. Get a good close-up of ME now. Get a good profile shot. Be sure to get my BETTER SIDE! Hahahaha!"

Kelly's hands shook as she pointed the camera at him.

"Know my better side?" Slappy rasped. *"The OUTside! Hahaha!"*

"Is that a joke?" Snappy asked.

"YOU'RE a joke!" Slappy cried. He swung back to Kelly. *"Keep filming. Keep filming. Know what I've decided to call this movie?* The Boy in the Glass Coffin. *Catchy, huh?"*

Without warning, he rushed forward, stretched out his arms—and grabbed me around the waist. Tightening his wooden hands around me, he hoisted me off the floor. He had such incredible strength, it was like he was raising a feather.

"Let GO!" I screamed. "Put me down!"

I thrashed my arms wildly and swung my legs hard, trying to kick him.

"*Snappy, get over here. Don't stand there like a dummy. Grab his legs. Help me. Grab his legs!*"

Snappy sighed and shook his head. But then he strode up to me, grabbed my legs, and held them tightly together.

"Let GO!" I screamed. "What are you doing? Let GO of me!"

I squirmed and twisted, but they were too strong. They carried me across the floor to the open display case.

"*Are you filming this?*" Slappy shouted to Kelly. "*This is AWESOME! What a killer scene! Don't miss this!*"

"*Be gentle, Slappy,*" his twin scolded. "*You don't want to hurt him.*"

"*I'll hurt YOU if you spoil this dynamite scene!*" Slappy cried.

The two dummies held me high over the glass case, then lowered me into it.

"No! No way!" I cried.

But before I could climb out, they lowered the lid over my head.

"You can't do this! Let me out—now!" I screamed, pounding on the glass wall.

Slappy fiddled with the lock. I heard it click. Then he tossed the key away.

"Let me OUT!" I screamed. I pounded on the glass with both fists.

I could feel my face turning red. I tried to swallow but couldn't. It felt as if my heart had jumped into my throat. Through the glass, I saw Kelly frozen with the little video camera still raised.

"I love it! Let's see some real terror now, Luke!" Slappy cried. *"Bang on the glass. That's good. Lots of feeling. Okay. Scream, Kelly. Let's hear it. Sell it! I smell an Academy Award performance! Keep beating the glass, Luke. You're red in the face now. Excellent. I'm loving it. Love that panic. Keep screaming. Keep pounding. Keep up the panic, everybody! Hahahahaha!"*

15

Gasping for air, I stopped beating my fists against the glass wall. I held my breath and tried to force my heart to stop beating so hard and fast against my chest. Sweat poured down my face.

I hunched on my knees, the lid just an inch or two above my head. The air quickly became hot in the glass case. Despite the heat, I felt cold chills at the back of my neck.

Through the glass, I saw Kelly finally lower the little camera. Her eyes were wide with fright. She gazed at me, then turned back to Slappy.

"Let him out! Why are you doing this?" she demanded in a trembling voice.

"Because I can do whatever I want!" the dummy replied. *"Did you forget? I'm Slappy!"*

"Don't brag," Snappy said softly. *"It isn't nice to brag."*

Slappy gave his twin a two-handed push. *"I'll try to be more polite, Snappy,"* he said. *"Is there a polite way to tell you to shut your wooden trap?"*

"*That hurts my feelings,*" Snappy replied.

Slappy tilted his head back and laughed. Then he turned back to Kelly. "*Your father likes horror movies. We'll see how he likes THIS one!*"

"You have to let my brother out of there!" Kelly declared.

Slappy shook his head. "*The only thing I have to do is destroy your father. First, Snappy and I are going to frighten him. Then we're going to ruin his film. Then we're going to ruin his LIFE!*"

"You . . . you . . . can't do that. You can't hurt my dad," Kelly stammered.

"*Oh, yes I can.*" Slappy cackled. "*He thinks he's going to sell us to two different collectors. He thinks he's going to split us up. I'm afraid Mr. Harrison, the big movie director, will have to pay for that idea!*"

"But . . . you and Snappy don't even *like* each other!" Kelly cried.

"*Mainly, I don't like YOU!*" Slappy growled.

I pressed my face against the glass wall of the display case. "Kelly, run downstairs!" I called. "Get Dad! Hurry!" But she didn't hear me.

Instead of trying to get to the attic stairs, Kelly lurched at Slappy. She wrapped her hands around his head and tried to slam him to the floor.

But he was too strong for her. He ducked low and pulled his head free. Then he shot forward and gave her a hard head butt. I could hear the *craaaack* of the collision through the glass.

Kelly groaned and sank to the floor on her knees. Slappy came at her and swung his shoe hard in a vicious kick. She dodged to the right, and his foot sailed over her shoulder.

With another loud groan, she grabbed his leg, pulled it with all her strength—and the dummy clattered to the floor.

Snappy stood frozen, watching the fight, half-hidden behind a tall display case. I silently urged Kelly to get up. Get up and run downstairs.

And to my surprise, she did it. Slappy's legs had tangled. He twisted his body, struggling to climb to his feet.

Kelly jumped over him and took off for the stairs.

"Come back!" Slappy called after her. *"The scene isn't over. The horror is just beginning! Hahaha!"*

Kelly vanished down the stairs. I hunched on my hands and knees. And waited. Waited for her to bring Dad.

The air was growing thin inside the case. My breath had steamed one side of the glass. I was drenched in a cold sweat.

The two dummies stood against the wall, ignoring me. They were arguing. Their big wooden hands flew in the air in front of them as they shouted at each other.

Hurry, Dad. Please hurry, I thought. *It's getting hard to breathe in here. Please hurry.*

Finally, I heard footsteps coming up the stairs. Kelly came bursting into the attic. Dad followed, moving slowly, still half-asleep, fiddling with the belt on his bathrobe.

He took a few steps. Then he stopped, and his eyes bulged when he saw me in the glass case.

"Dad—*now* do you believe us?" Kelly cried.

16

Dad didn't move. Maybe he thought he was still asleep and dreaming the whole scene. He squinted hard at me.

"What on earth—" he muttered finally.

Then he lowered his eyes to the floor and stepped back in surprise.

I saw what he was staring at. The two dummies. They were tangled up, in a lifeless heap on the floor against the wall. Dad pushed one in the back with his bare foot. It flopped limply against the floor.

"Do you see?" Kelly cried, pointing a trembling finger at me in the glass case. "Dad—you see what they did to Luke? You believe us now—right?"

Dad rubbed his beard with both hands. "Kelly, get serious," he said. "Did you really think you could fool me with this trick?"

Kelly's mouth dropped open. "Huh? Trick?"

Dad poked the dummy again with his toe. "You really want me to believe that these dummies put Luke in the case? Look at them, Kelly. They're not alive. They don't move on their own."

"But, Dad—"

"If you wanted to fool me," Dad said, "why didn't you at least stand the dummies up? Why did you toss them in a heap on the floor?" He scowled. "Now, let's get your brother out of there before he suffocates. Where's the key?"

Kelly blinked. "I don't know. Slappy threw it across the room."

"*Stop it, Kelly!*" Dad screamed. Dad is such a quiet guy, it's always a shock when he raises his voice. Kelly actually jumped. "No more dummy talk," Dad said. "Find the key."

Kelly scrambled down the row of display cases. She dropped to her knees and began searching the floor.

Dad stepped up to the case and peered in at me. "Are you okay?" he asked. "This was a really stupid thing to do." He shook his head. "You two are supposed to be smart. Why on earth did you decide to play these stupid dummy games?"

They're not games, I thought. *The twin dummies are really out to teach Dad a lesson. They are dangerous.*

We had to convince Dad before they did something really horrible. But how?

"Found it!" Kelly shouted from across the attic. She came running over with the key in her hand.

A few seconds later, I was out of the glass case, legs trembling, drenched in sweat, breathing hard, my chest moving in and out like an accordion.

Dad put a hand on my shoulder. "Promise me you'll never pull a stupid stunt like this again."

"It wasn't a stunt!" Kelly's jaw clenched. She only did that when she was furiously angry. "Dad, you have *got* to believe us."

She grabbed the GoPro camera and shoved it into his hands. "Check this out. It's all on video. Watch it, Dad. Then it's your turn to apologize to Luke and me."

Dad fumbled the camera between his hands. Then he raised it close and studied the screen. Squinting hard, he pressed a button. Then another.

He raised his eyes to Kelly. "It's blank. There's nothing here."

Kelly let out a cry of disgust and slapped her forehead. "Luke—" she shouted. "Did you forget to press the RECORD button?"

She was right. I never pressed it.

Just kill me now, I thought.

Dad tucked the camera into his bathrobe pocket. "You promised there wouldn't be one more dummy incident," Dad said. "Remember? You and your brother promised, Kelly."

"But, Dad—"

"So . . . I have no choice. You two are off the movie. You have to break it to your friend Jamal. You're not going to the set. You're not going to be in the film."

A few minutes later, I climbed into bed. Even though it was a warm night, I pulled the covers up to my chin. My body was still shaking, and my brain was whirring with angry and frightening thoughts.

Thoughts about the two dummies and their plan to ruin Dad.

Thoughts about how Dad might never trust Kelly and me again.

He said we were acting stupid.

And now we can't be in the movie.

I sat up, turned, and punched my pillow hard. I had to punch something!

I was still sitting up when I heard the sounds from my bedroom window. The window was open, and I could see the pale yellow light of a full moon, low in the night sky.

I listened. It sounded like someone giggling. Shrill laughter.

I nearly tripped and fell, tangled in my bedsheet, as I bolted to the window. I peered down to the backyard. And there they were.

The two dummies. Slappy and Snappy. Clapping their hands above their heads, twisting and turning and kicking. Doing a wild, crazy dance under the moonlight.

Were they celebrating their victory over Kelly and me?

I watched them dance for a few seconds. Then I turned and raced out into the hall.

Dad had a glass of juice in his hand. He was about to go into his bedroom.

"Dad!" I screamed. "Hurry! Come fast!" I motioned with both hands for him to follow me to my room.

He hesitated. I rushed forward, grabbed his arm, almost spilling the juice. I tugged him into my room. Up to the window. "Look!" I cried.

"Just look." I tilted his head down.

Then I peered down to the yard beside him.

The two dummies were gone.

17

The next morning, a Saturday, Dad was already dressed and setting the breakfast table when Kelly and I came downstairs. We were yawning and droopy and sleepy-eyed. I know I hadn't slept much, and I bet Kelly hadn't, either.

"Listen, Dad—" I started.

But he raised a hand to silence me. "No time for any discussions this morning," he said. "I'm having an important breakfast meeting here. I asked Lucy to set up your breakfast on the patio by the pool."

Lucy is our housekeeper. She has her own apartment in the guest house on the other side of our swimming pool.

"Who's coming?" I asked, yawning.

"Simon Benedict," Dad said. "He's the exec producer of my last four films. Know what that means? It means he puts up the money. He pays for everything."

"So you want to impress him?" Kelly said. She picked up a fork and twirled it between her fingers.

Dad took the fork from her and returned it to the napkin it had been placed on. "I don't have to impress Simon," he said. "We've known each other a long time, and I've made a lot of money for him."

Dad smiled. "But I *do* want to stay on his good side."

Kelly and I made our way to the patio. "Dad *does* want to impress this guy," Kelly whispered. "He *never* makes breakfast for anyone here at the house."

I followed her out the back door. It was a beautiful, warm, cloudless Los Angeles morning. The trees shimmered on the hills around our house, and the air smelled sweet like flowers.

A squirrel stared at us from the center of the patio. It was eyeing a nut on a lounge chair cushion. The nut must have fallen from one of the fruit trees that overhangs the patio.

The pool glistened like silver, reflecting the morning sun above us.

I turned when a shadow caught my eye. A slender blue-black shadow at the edge of the house. I grabbed Kelly's shoulder. "Look."

We both gazed at the two dummies. They leaned against the redwood shingles at the back wall of the house, half-hidden in shade. They were watching us.

"I don't believe it," I muttered.

Kelly opened her mouth to reply, but stopped. Slappy was motioning with one hand, waving us over.

We both hesitated. But we knew we couldn't ignore them. We had no choice. We had to find out what they wanted.

I turned back and looked for Lucy. Did she see them, too?

No. Lucy had put out our breakfast on the glass table by the pool and had gone back inside.

I took a deep breath and led the way toward the dummies. When we came close, they grabbed us by the arms and tugged us out of sight, around to the side of the house.

"What are you doing out here?" I demanded, jerking my arm free. "What do you want?"

"Do you want us to leave?" Slappy rasped, his glassy green eyes reflecting the sun, making them appear on fire. *"Do you want Snappy and me to leave? I'll tell you how you can do it."*

18

"Is this a joke?" Kelly asked. "Are you serious?"

"*I'm serious,*" Slappy said, his jaw clicking as it moved up and down.

Snappy nodded but didn't speak.

"*You do one thing for me. And my brother and I will disappear, and you'll never see us again,*" Slappy said.

Kelly and I just stared at them. My brain was spinning. Could we really get rid of these two frightening pests?

"If we do what you say . . . you'll really just leave?" Kelly said.

Both dummies nodded. "*We can't wait to get out of here,*" Slappy said.

"But you said you wanted to ruin our dad," Kelly said.

"*Forget all that,*" Slappy replied. "*You do one thing for us, and we're outta here. I swear.*" He raised his right hand.

Kelly and I exchanged glances. We were both

thinking the same question: What horrible thing did they want us to do?

"*Will you do it?*" Slappy asked.

"*Slappy, say* please," Snappy chimed in.

"*Will you do it?*" Slappy repeated, ignoring him.

"Depends," I said.

"*It isn't dangerous,*" Slappy said. "*No one will get hurt. It's kind of a joke. You'll see. It's funny.*"

He handed me a small black earbud. "*Slip that in your ear, Luke.*"

I held it between my fingers and examined it. "Where did you get this?"

"*From your father's equipment room,*" Slappy replied. "*I just borrowed it. Go ahead. Put it in your ear.*"

I studied it some more. Then I pushed it into my right ear.

"*It's a tiny speaker,*" Slappy explained. "*I'm going to speak into your ear. You'll be able to hear me clearly.*"

"And what do I do?" I demanded.

"*You just repeat everything I say,*" Slappy explained. "*It's so simple, even a dummy like YOU can understand it.*"

"*Be polite,*" Snappy scolded.

Slappy raised his wooden hand and gave Snappy a hard slap on the head. "*Is that polite enough for you?*"

Kelly shook her head. "This sounds like a bad idea," she said softly.

"I promise no one will get hurt," Slappy repeated. *"Your father's guest, Mr. Benedict, has arrived. Luke, you go in and say hello to him. Then repeat everything I say.* Everything, *do you understand?"*

"And then what?" I said.

"Then Snappy and I will disappear. You will be rid of us. And you will have saved your dad a lot of pain and trouble."

"This is too good to be true," Kelly whispered.

"I'll do it," I whispered back. "It's worth a try. If it means we can save Dad from these two."

I turned to Slappy. "Okay. I'll do it."

"Good boy," Slappy said. His eyes flashed. *"Remember. Repeat everything I say. Don't leave anything out. If you don't follow my instruction, Snappy and I will stay here. And I promise you won't be happy."*

I turned and started toward the back door. "Come on, Kelly. Let's go."

Slappy grabbed Kelly's wrist. "No. She stays here. You're on your own."

"Luke—are you sure you want to do this?" Kelly asked, trying to pull away.

I swallowed. "Do I have a choice?"

19

I walked into the breakfast room. Dad and Mr. Benedict were just settling down at the table. Dad was pouring orange juice from a silver pitcher.

Mr. Benedict was wearing a dark gray suit jacket over jeans. He had a pale T-shirt under the jacket. He was bald and his head was sort of light bulb shaped. He was very tanned, which made his blue eyes appear to glow. He had a silver ring in one ear and gray stubble on his cheeks.

He took a sip of orange juice, then smiled as I walked in.

"Simon, this is my son, Luke," Dad said. He squinted at me. "Luke, did you finish your breakfast already?"

Before I could answer, I heard Slappy's voice in my ear. He said: *Repeat after me. Mr. Benedict, is that a huge ugly wart on your shoulders, or is that your head?*

"Oh." I groaned.

"*Go ahead. Repeat it,*" Slappy ordered, his voice tinny in the little earbud.

"Mr. Benedict," I said, "Is that a huge ugly wart on your shoulders, or is that your head?"

Benedict blinked. He twisted his face in confusion. I could see he didn't really believe what he heard.

"*Repeat after me,*" Slappy said in my ear. "*Is that your nose, or are you eating a cucumber?*"

"Is that your nose, or are you eating a cucumber?" I repeated.

Benedict's cheeks turned pink. He turned to my dad. "David, I didn't know your son was a comedian."

"I—I didn't, either," Dad stammered. "Luke—what's the big idea?"

"*Dad says your nickname is Walrus Butt. Is that true?*" Slappy said.

I choked. I almost gagged.

"*Repeat it,*" Slappy ordered. "*You want to save your dad from me—don't you? You want me to go away forever?*"

"Dad says your nickname is Walrus Butt. Is that true?" I said.

My stomach lurched. I felt sick. I lowered my eyes. I couldn't bear to see the angry look on Mr. Benedict's face.

Dad's chair scraped the floor as he jumped to his feet. "I'm sorry, Simon," he said. "Luke has never done this before. I apologize for him."

Dad grabbed my shoulder. "Luke, this isn't funny."

Slappy's voice rang in my ear: *"Dad says your IQ is the same as your belt size."*

"Dad says your IQ is the same as your belt size," I repeated. I felt as if I'd left my own body, and someone else was saying these things.

"Dad told us you give crooks a bad name."

"Dad told us you give crooks a bad name."

"Luke—stop!" Dad screamed.

Benedict was on his feet now. His face looked like a red light bulb, and he was breathing hard. "Talk later, David," he said to my father. He took long strides to the front door and didn't look back.

"Simon, wait—" Dad called.

But the door slammed behind Benedict. He was gone.

Dad held me by the shoulders. "What was that about, Luke? What's *wrong* with you? Why did you do that?"

My head was spinning. My stomach felt as if a roller coaster was going up and down inside it. "Dad, it—it was the dummies," I stammered.

"NO!" he boomed. "No, Luke. No dummy story."

I pulled the earbud from my ear. "Slappy said those things and made me repeat them."

Dad took it from my hand. He held it to his ear. Of course, it was silent now.

He sighed. "I don't know what to do about you. I'm really stumped."

"They're out on the patio," I said. "Both of them. Slappy and Snappy. Kelly will tell you. I'm not making it up."

Dad didn't say a word. He spun away from me and started toward the back door. I hurried after him.

We stepped outside. Kelly was sitting at the table, tapping a foot nervously, waiting for me to return. She waved from the other side of the pool. Lucy was coming out of the pool house, carrying a stack of towels.

I tugged Dad's arm. "They're over here, Dad. Around the side of the house."

I pulled Dad around the corner. No one there. The dummies were gone.

Dad shook his head. I suddenly realized he was more sad than angry. He must have thought I was going wacko.

I ran back to the patio. "Kelly—where did the dummies go?" I shouted.

She shrugged. "I don't know. They told me to stay here."

"Why are you and your sister playing this dumb game?" Dad asked. "What do you hope to gain? I have no choice, Luke. I have to ground you."

I bit my bottom lip. "It's not a game, Dad. Kelly and I are trying to *save* you."

"Ha! That's a good one," Dad said. "Save me by insulting the producer of my movie? By making up crazy stories? You're frightening me, Luke. I'm being very honest with you. You and your sister are frightening me."

"But, Dad—"

"Not another word," he said. "Follow me. Now." He started back into the house.

"Dad, where are we going?"

"Just follow me." We walked past the breakfast room. The food for his breakfast meeting with Simon Benedict sat uneaten on the table. Dad sighed as we passed it and turned into the back hall.

We climbed the attic stairs and stepped into the attic. Morning sunlight poured into the windows, sending bright beams of light over the display cases.

"Look," Dad said. He stopped in front of the glass case at the end.

The two dummies were inside, sprawled lifelessly on their backs. Their legs were folded beneath them. Their arms hung limply at their sides. Their big eyes gazed blankly up at the low attic ceiling.

"Big surprise," Dad said. "They haven't moved from this case, Luke."

"Dad, listen—"

"No. I don't have time to listen. Help me carry

these dummies downstairs. I have a special van coming to take them to the studio. This morning is the first day of filming. And I'm very sorry you and Kelly and Jamal won't be joining us."

Dad unlocked the case, and we lifted the dummies out. I slung Slappy over my shoulder and followed Dad to the stairs. I walked slowly. I let Dad get ahead.

I stopped at the top of the stairs and waited till Dad was all the way down. Then I lifted Slappy's head and whispered: "You promised! You promised if I did what you said, you and your brother would disappear. You promised!"

The dummy's eyes blinked open. The ugly grin appeared to grow wider. *"Hahahahaha!"* he laughed. *"I'm a dirty liar!"*

SLAPPY HERE, EVERYONE.

Hahaha. I told you the best way to spell Luke's name. Why did he believe me in the first place? Only a dummy would believe a dummy. Haha. It turns out that Luke is the one with sawdust for brains! Hahaha.

Actually, I'm an honest dude. I *always* tell the truth. Unless I can think of a good lie! Ha.

I loved it when he called Simon Benedict *Walrus Butt*. Haha. Hope I didn't offend any walruses in the audience. If I did . . . *tusk tusk*.

Ha. Let's get back to Luke's story. Guess what? It gets even scarier.

Big surprise?

20

Later that afternoon, Kelly, Jamal, and I were in the garage, working on our drone project. The propellers were harder to connect than anyone thought. Jamal thought we had the wrong bolts.

"But they're the bolts that came with the kit," I argued.

He scrunched up his face. "That doesn't mean they're the *right* bolts."

Kelly sighed. "Dad has probably started filming now. I can't believe we're not there."

"I can't believe it, either," Jamal said, shaking his head. "My one chance to be in a movie." He let the propeller in his hand drop to the garage floor. "Know what else I don't believe?"

I turned to him. "You don't believe in the Tooth Fairy?"

"Remind me to laugh," he said. "I don't believe your father doesn't believe *us*. Does he really think we are total liars?"

"Yes, he does," I said. "Would *you* believe us? The whole dummy thing is too crazy to believe."

"I wouldn't believe it, either," Kelly said. "And we weren't able to prove it to Dad. We failed every time we thought we had proof."

Jamal shook his head again. His dark hair flopped over his forehead. "But . . . it isn't right. Doesn't he trust you two at all?"

"Jamal, you have to understand one thing," I said. "Dad is in the movie business. People tell him wild stories all the time."

"But . . . we were trying to *help* him," Jamal said. "Those dummies want to hurt him. They want to *ruin* his movie."

"You know it, and I know it," I replied. "But Dad doesn't know it."

"Dad won't listen to us no matter what," Kelly said. She picked up the steel propeller and pushed it into Jamal's hands. "Come on. We want to finish this thing and fly it, don't we?"

Jamal bent down and grabbed a handful of the long metal bolts from the floor. "You two hold the propeller in place. Let me see . . ."

Kelly and I raised the propeller over the frame.

Jamal dropped a bolt into one of the holes in the steel. Then he lowered the propeller onto the frame. "Hmm . . . Maybe . . ." he muttered.

Then he stopped.

And his eyes bulged in surprise.

"Hey—" he cried. "Whoa. I mean—whoa."

I turned toward the back of the garage. I tried to follow his gaze. "I—I don't see anything," I stammered.

"That's the point," Jamal said, still wide-eyed. "I don't see anything, either."

"What do you mean?" Kelly demanded.

"The propane tank," Jamal said. "Where is it? It's gone."

"Ohhh." A moan escaped my throat. I stared at the spot near the wall where the big tank had stood. Then my eyes quickly swept the whole garage. "Yes. Gone," I murmured.

Kelly grabbed my arm. "You don't think—?"

"The dummies," I said. "Is it possible? The dummies were being taken to the studio in a large van. Do you think they took the propane tank along with them?" A shudder ran down my whole body.

"They're going to blow up your dad's studio," Jamal said. "Don't you see? People could get *killed*! We have to do something!"

21

I grabbed my phone. "I'll text Dad. I'll warn him."

Kelly frowned at me. "Like he'll believe you?"

"I'll call him and explain," I said.

"He'll probably laugh," Jamal said.

"Or he'll get even angrier at us," Kelly added. "Dad doesn't believe the dummies are alive, Luke. So he won't believe anything we say about them taking the propane tank. He'll think *we* put it in the van."

"He's *got* to believe," Jamal said. "We have to *make* him believe."

I tried to swallow but my mouth was as dry as cotton. "Dad could be killed," I said, my voice cracking on the words. "A lot of people could be killed. I have no choice. I have to try to reach him."

My hand trembled. I nearly dropped the phone. I brought the phone close to my face and texted Dad:

Need to talk to you. Urgent.

Then I held the phone up and waited for a reply.

And waited.

And waited some more.

"Try calling," Jamal said.

I squinted at the screen, found Dad's number, and punched it in.

The phone went straight to his voicemail:

"This is David Harrison. Leave a message."

"Dad, where are you?" I said after the beep. "Call us. It's really important."

"He's probably on the set," Kelly said. "Maybe he started filming already. He won't see his phone. He'll be too busy."

"We have to go there," Jamal said. "We have to go to the studio. Maybe we can warn him in time."

"Don't say *maybe*," I said. "We have no choice. We *have* to warn him in time."

"But how do we get there?" Kelly said. "We can't walk to Burbank."

"A taxi?" I said. "Do you have any money?"

"I have a taxi app on my phone," Jamal said. "My parents gave it to me to come home from my cello lessons." He pulled out his phone and started typing, calling for a car. "It will be here in seven minutes," he said.

I was so tense, I was hopping up and down. "What do we do for seven minutes?"

"Worry?" Kelly answered.

"Sounds like a plan," I said. "Or maybe . . ." I

tried Dad's number again. Again, it went straight to voicemail.

I texted again.

No reply.

We waited in the driveway for the car, and the driver pulled up in a red Toyota about ten minutes later.

The ride from our house in the Hollywood Hills to Dad's studio in Burbank is about half an hour. I usually think it's exciting to drive past the Warner Brothers lot and Disney Studios. But today, everything outside the car window was just a blur.

The three of us didn't say a word the whole way there. I kept trying to call Dad, but he didn't answer.

We directed the driver to the Horror House Films parking lot. "Pull into that driveway," I said. "We have to stop at the security booth."

I rolled down my window when we pulled up to the little round booth. A guard in a dark blue uniform and cap leaned out. He had long gray hair falling from the cap. He wore thick eyeglasses that glinted in the sun.

He must have been new. I'd never seen him before.

"We need to see David Harrison," I said.

He pulled out a long clipboard. "Name?"

"Luke Harrison. I'm his son. And that's my sister, Kelly, and our friend Jamal."

He studied the clipboard.

My heart was pounding. "We're kind of in a hurry," I said.

He raised his eyes to me. "I don't see your names on the list."

"I know," I said, feeling panic rise up in my chest. "He isn't expecting us. But I told you, he's our dad."

He stared at me through the thick eyeglasses. "I can't really let anyone in unless their name is on the list."

That's when I lost it. "I'm his *son*!" I screamed. "*I need to see my dad!*"

Our driver ducked his head. I think my shout startled him.

The parking guard checked his clipboard again. He picked up a phone. "I'll try to reach him." He squinted at me. "What is your name again?"

I gritted my teeth. "Luke Harrison."

He pushed some numbers on his phone and listened. Then he poked his head out of the booth again. "No one is answering."

My throat tightened. "You're not going to let us in?"

"Sorry, but I could lose my job. You have to be on the list."

"But we're just kids!" I cried. "You have to—"

He shook his head. "I'm sorry. Seriously. I'm real sorry."

22

Kelly, Jamal, and I sat in the car staring out at him. I couldn't believe this was happening. The other guards all knew Kelly and me because we always arrived with Dad.

This was crazy. We were so close . . .

Suddenly Jamal spoke up. He leaned over the seat and whispered to the driver. "Ask him if you can pull in and turn around."

It took me a few seconds to figure out what Jamal had in mind. Beside me, Kelly tensed. She figured it out, too.

The guard waved the driver into the parking lot. "Just make a circle and come back out."

The driver nodded. He pulled the car inside and made a wide circle, stopping at the side door to the offices. "Hurry. Before he sees you," he said.

Kelly, Jamal, and I jumped out. We watched him pull away, then we slipped through the door into the building.

Jamal rolled his eyes. "That was easy."

I peered down the long hallway. No one in sight. The building was very modern looking. Bright blue-and-yellow walls. Tall bronze sculptures. Glass office doors. Lots of sunlight streamed in from high windows.

"This way," I said. I was pretty sure I could find Dad's office. We had to find Ms. Duveen, Dad's secretary. She'd know where Dad was filming. We started to trot, our shoes thudding the hard floor.

We passed large framed posters of the movies Dad had made here. *The 800-Pound Gorilla . . . Octo-Man vs. the Squid Sisters . . . It Came from Beneath My Bed . . .*

"These are awesome," Jamal said, stopping to admire the big poster for *Jaws of the Jellyfish.* "I never saw that one."

I gave him a gentle shove. "Keep going. We have to find Dad, remember? A little problem about a propane tank?"

We stopped short when two young men in jeans and polo shirts crossed the hall ahead of us. They were both talking at once, waving papers in their hands, and didn't see us.

I realized my heart was thudding in my chest. Was I leading in the right direction?

I heard some women laughing in an office to our left. "Hurry," I whispered. We ran past the office and turned a corner. It suddenly looked familiar. In front of us, there stood an enormous eight-foot-tall gold Oscar award with a hairy gorilla arm coming out of the top. That's what greeted visitors to the studio.

I knew Dad's office was on the other side of the statue. I could see the double glass doors at the end of the hall. I took off running. I could hear Kelly and Jamal close behind.

I pushed open the glass door and burst inside. Ms. Duveen wasn't at her desk. The door to Dad's office was open behind it.

I swerved around Ms. Duveen's desk and poked my head into Dad's office. His desk was piled high with papers, mostly scripts. A younger Kelly and I grinned at ourselves from a framed photo on the wall.

"We have to get to the set before the dummies do their dirty work," I said.

"But how do we find it?" Jamal asked.

"Wait. I think I know," I said. "I think it's in that huge building that looks like an airplane hangar, behind these offices."

So we took off again, with me leading the way. I have to admit that I don't spend a lot of time running. I'm not on any sports teams, and I don't jog or run for fun. So all this running was making me gasp for breath. My leg muscles throbbed, and I had a sharp pain in my side.

But I knew we might not have much time. We had to get to Dad as fast as we could. We turned into another long hall that led to the back of the building.

About eight or nine people were seated around a long table in a conference room. They all turned and looked up as we went running past.

"Who are those kids?" I heard a woman ask.

I didn't hear the answer, because Kelly, Jamal, and I pushed open the doors and ran onto the back lot.

I could see the maroon hangar-like building across a wide plaza. Men were moving a tall boom microphone in through the front doors. Several people stood at the side of the entrance, talking and waving scripts in their hands.

In front of us stood a row of white trailers. I knew the actors stayed in their trailers when they weren't working on the set. And I knew there were trailers for the makeup people, and a few trailers for the tech guys.

Almost there, I thought. In a few seconds, we'd be at the set and we could tell Dad about the missing propane tank—and maybe save everyone's lives.

"This way." I motioned to Kelly and Jamal. They were both breathing hard. And I could see the tension on their faces as they gazed at the enormous building.

We started to run through the rows of trailers when a voice rang out:

"Hey—stop!"

With a sharp gasp, I turned to see two dark-uniformed security guards moving toward us.

"The guy in the parking lot," Jamal choked out. "He must have alerted them."

"Stop! Stop right there, kids."

"You don't belong on this lot!"

The two men began jogging fast.

We slipped between two trailers, where they couldn't see us.

We had to escape. We had to find Dad. We didn't have time to deal with these guards.

My brain was spinning. I didn't think. There was no time to think.

I ran up the short ladder, pulled open the door to one of the trailers. And the three of us stumbled inside.

23

Jamal slammed the door shut behind him.

Dark inside. The trailer's one window was covered by a shade.

Was anyone in here? I couldn't hear anything over my wheezing breaths. My heart felt as if it had jumped into my mouth, and I could barely breathe.

The three of us stood frozen in the darkness. Listening. Listening to the shouts of the guards outside the trailer. They ran past us. I could hear the heavy thuds of their shoes on the pavement. Their shouts grew fainter.

We didn't move till we were sure they were gone. Then I fumbled on the wall, found a light switch, and clicked on a ceiling light.

No one else in here. The trailer had two canvas director chairs, a low table with a six-pack of water bottles, a mini-refrigerator against the wall. A red metal lunchbox on the floor beside a stack of books. A plate of cookies and a bowl of fruit.

"Oh no!"

Kelly was the first to see them.

Her cry made me spin around. And I saw them, too.

The two dummies. Slappy and Snappy. They had been hung on the wall on large hooks. Their arms and legs fell limply down. Their heads were down, too, slumped so we could see only their dark, painted hair.

"This is where they are storing them," Jamal said.

"We got lucky," Kelly said. "Maybe we can make them talk."

A burst of anger made me feel hot all over. A roar escaped my throat. We had these two evil troublemakers alone.

I lurched forward and grabbed the dummy on the left. I pulled him off the hook, turned his head, and stared at his eyes. Green eyes. Slappy.

My anger took over. I held the dummy by the waist and shook him hard, shook him with all my strength.

"*Tell* us!" I screamed. "Tell us—now. Where did you put the propane tank? Talk!"

Slappy's head bobbed back and forth as I shook him. His wooden eyelids opened and closed. His feet dangled crazily, doing a wild dance in the air as I jerked him one way, then the other.

"Talk!" I screamed. "Where is it?"

The dummy's head bobbed lifelessly. It didn't speak.

Kelly leaped forward and grabbed Slappy by the head. She twisted it until the eyes stared at her. "We know you have the tank," she said. "And we know you're planning something terrible. Tell us where it is, Slappy."

The eyes gazed glassily at her. The mouth didn't move.

I took the dummy by the legs and swung it hard. Its head hit the trailer wall with a loud *thunnnk*. "Tell us!" I cried.

Slappy remained limp and silent.

"He's not going to tell us," Jamal said. "Let's try the other dummy."

He lifted Snappy off the hook and lowered the dummy in front of him. "Snappy, you're the good brother," Jamal said. "You are the sensible one, the kind one. You've *got* to tell us where Slappy has hidden the propane tank."

Silence. The dummy drooped in his arms, its shoes tapping against the floor.

"Snappy, come on," Kelly insisted. "You have to stop your brother. You don't want him to harm innocent people—do you?"

No response.

I shook Slappy some more. "Are you going to speak up?"

"I know you two don't want my dad to split

100

you up," Kelly told Snappy. "But you don't want to let Slappy blow up the whole studio—do you?"

We were getting nowhere. The two dummies were acting like lifeless puppets. We knew the truth. We knew they could speak. And we knew they had brought the propane tank and hidden it somewhere.

I was so angry and frightened and frustrated, I began to twist Slappy's arm. "How does that feel? Can you feel that? Does it hurt?"

Kelly grabbed my hand. "Stop, Luke. It isn't working. We have to find Dad."

A loud *clannnk* from the trailer door as it opened made all three of us jump. Slappy fell from my hands and crumpled in a heap at my feet.

A bright beam of sunlight slanted into the trailer as the door started to open.

"The guards. We're caught!" I whispered.

24

The young man who climbed into the trailer didn't look like a security guard. He had curly black hair falling from beneath a Dodgers baseball cap, and a black beard. He wore silvery sunglasses, baggy denim jeans, and a red-and-black flannel lumberjack shirt open over a black T-shirt.

His mouth dropped open when he saw the three of us. He pulled off his sunglasses and squinted at us. "Who are you? What are you doing in here?" he demanded. He had a soft, whispery voice.

"My dad owns the studio," I said. "Have you seen him?"

He rubbed his beard. "No. I just got here. But you didn't answer my question."

"It's a long story," I said. "These dummies—"

"Who are *you*?" Kelly interrupted. "Is this your trailer?"

"Kind of," he answered. "My name is Derek.

I'm the puppeteer. I'm going to be operating these two guys."

"They don't *need* a puppeteer," Jamal chimed in. "They walk and talk on their own."

"Ha," Derek said. "Funny."

"No. We're serious," Kelly said, still holding on to Snappy. "We're not joking."

"I think I saw some horror movies like that," Derek said. "Did you ever see the Chucky movies? Or are you too young?" He bent to pick Slappy up from the floor. "You shouldn't be playing with these things. I was told they are very valuable."

I grabbed Derek's arm. "Listen to me," I said. "We are trying to tell you the truth. These dummies are alive—and they are totally dangerous."

He grinned at me. "Thanks for the warning, dude. I'll try to be careful." Then he burst out laughing.

I let out a frustrated sigh. "Derek, did you see a propane tank anywhere?"

He rubbed his beard. "No. I told you. I just got here. I came straight from the parking lot."

He raised Slappy in front of him. "Listen, kids. It's been fun, but you've got to go. I have a two o'clock call. Got to rehearse these guys."

We were already heading to the trailer door. *No way* we could convince Derek that we were telling the truth about Slappy and Snappy. *No way* we could get him to believe how much trouble we were all in.

Jamal pushed open the door and jumped down the stairs. Kelly followed.

I was at the door, about to leave, when I turned back. And saw Slappy raise his head. His green eyes blinked and locked on me. His mouth opened. And he whispered, *"BOOOOOOM."*

25

We cut through the rows of trailers. I kept glancing one way, then the other, looking out for security guards. The afternoon sun was high in the sky now. There was no breeze at all. Drips of sweat covered my forehead and trickled into my eyes.

"Whoa. Stop," I whispered. I saw two dark-uniformed guards at the catering table at the side of the wide maroon studio building. They were piling sandwiches onto their plates.

A golf cart carrying three young women in light-colored business suits stopped at the entrance to the building. The three women climbed out and began talking with another guard at the door.

"We have to get in there," I said. "Look. That red light is on. It means they are shooting a scene."

"Dad must be in there," Kelly said. "Think the guard will let us past the door?"

"Maybe he will if you tell him who you are," Jamal said.

"And if we tell him it's an emergency," I added.

BOOM!

I screamed at the sound of an explosion.

My knees started to fold. I grabbed the side of a trailer to hold myself up.

It took a few seconds to realize it wasn't an explosion. Someone had dropped a giant metal wheel of cable off a truck, and it had hit the ground with a deafening bang.

My heart still pounding, I motioned Kelly and Jamal forward. The two security dudes had walked away with their sandwiches. Only a few people hung around outside the entrance to the studio.

"Act like we belong here," Jamal said. "Act like we know where we're going. Maybe we'll get in."

"Don't say *maybe*," Kelly said. "We've wasted a lot of time already. We don't know how much time we have. We *have* to get in there."

We made our way past the long food table. And we were just a few steps from the studio door—when a tall, blond woman in a dark skirt and bright blue top stepped quickly to block our path.

"Hey, what are you kids doing here? Did David invite you to be extras in the crowd scene today?"

"Hi, Ms. Duveen," I said. I recognized Dad's secretary instantly.

I could have answered *yes* to her question. But I didn't want to lie to her. I liked her a lot. "We—we have to see Dad right away," I stammered.

Ms. Duveen pointed to the red light. "You can't go in. They're shooting a scene in there now."

"But it's a matter of life or death!" Kelly cried.

Ms. Duveen shook her head. Her short blond hair gleamed in the bright sunlight. "It will be *your* death if you interrupt your dad's scene."

"You don't understand," I said. "There's danger. I mean, we're all in danger. I mean—"

Ms. Duveen raised her phone to her face. "Sorry, kids. I have to take this." She pressed the phone to her ear, turned, and walked off toward the side of the building.

"Let's go!" I cried. The guard had disappeared. The red light was still on. But we had no choice. This was our big chance.

I took a deep breath and tugged open the tall door. A deafening explosion of noise made me cry out. A clanging bell. It sounded like the fire alarm at school. We'd set off an alarm.

I heard Kelly and Jamal gasp. They both slipped in behind me.

I squinted into the bright lights and screamed over the wail of the shrill, clanging alarm. "Dad! Dad! Where are you? Dad?"

He wasn't there.

26

I shielded my eyes with one hand. The lights were blindingly bright. "Dad?"

My eyes focused on the people standing around a coffee shop set. I saw four actors, two teenage boys and two girls, seated in a booth. All four of them jumped to their feet, covering their ears from the blare of the alarm.

A woman dropped her clipboard and spun around to stare at us. Crew members backed away from the camera and sound equipment. People shook their heads and shouted to one another.

Jamal, Kelly, and I huddled together just inside the door. I knew we had caused all the commotion. I knew we had just interrupted a scene.

But what we had to tell Dad was a lot more important.

If only he were here!

And then I saw him. He stepped out from behind a round spotlight and came stomping toward us. He swung his fists at his sides as he strode across the set. He squinted at us. His expression seemed more confused than angry.

Someone cut the alarm off, and the huge hangar grew silent for a few seconds. Then it seemed as if everyone began to talk at once.

"Dad—" I started as he roared up to us.

But he didn't give me a chance to talk. "What are you doing here? You ruined the first good take of the day. I told you not to come. I'm not using you in the movie—remember?"

"We *had* to come," I shouted, my voice more shrill than I'd intended. My words echoed off the high walls. "This time, you have to listen to us, Dad."

"This time, someone could get hurt," Kelly added.

Dad slapped the sides of his head. "Don't tell me. You've got another crazy dummy story. *Please* don't tell me you're going to talk about those dummies."

Jamal cleared his throat. "You should give them a chance, Mr. Harrison."

Dad shook his head. "I swear I'll *kill* someone if you tell me you ruined my scene because of those dummies."

I grabbed Dad's arm. "Just listen to us. We're not crazy. And we're not stupid. This isn't a joke or a story."

"This is real," Kelly said. "You've got to believe us."

Dad pulled his arm free of my grip. "Okay. Go ahead. I'm giving you thirty seconds before we have a conversation about how much trouble you're in."

"*You're* the one who's in trouble," I said. "The dummies are alive, Dad—no matter what you say. And they took the big propane tank from the garage."

"They want to ruin your movie, Mr. Harrison," Jamal said. "They're going to blow up this building. People will get hurt. Maybe even killed."

"You've *got* to believe us," Kelly pleaded.

Dad crossed his arms over his chest. He had a scowl on his face. His eyes moved from Kelly to Jamal to me. "Let's say the dummies really are alive," he said. "Why on earth would they want to blow up my studio? Can you explain that?"

"Yes, we can," I said. "They don't want you to sell them to different owners and split them up."

Dad scratched his beard. "Very good story idea for a horror movie," he said.

"But do you believe us now?" I demanded. "Do you believe we're telling the truth?"

His scowl grew deeper. "No, I don't believe you," he said. "I don't believe a single word of it. And you three are in the worst trouble you've ever been in your lives."

I uttered a choking sound. "But—why, Dad?" I cried.

He shook his head. "Because the dummies didn't take the propane tank. I did."

27

People were moving all around the enormous studio. Sliding lights and sound equipment into place . . . rehearsing in small groups . . . talking and arguing . . . standing around, eating sandwiches and drinking coffee.

But Dad's words made everything freeze in front of me in a flash of white light.

I don't know how long I stood there, blinking at my dad, trying to understand what he had just told us . . . Trying to make my brain sta.t working again.

Finally, it was Jamal who broke the silence. "Y-you took the tank?" he stuttered.

Dad nodded. "Yes, I did. I was afraid the tank was too close to the house. So I moved it in back of the garage."

I blinked a few more times. I've heard about people in shock. I guess this was what it felt like.

Dad narrowed his eyes at me. "No dummies coming to life, Luke. No dummies plotting against me . . . planning to blow up my studio. Do you see why I don't believe your horror story? Do you see why I'm angry that you tried to fool me? That you came here with that wild, insane plot and ruined my scene this afternoon?"

"I—I—" I stammered. I glanced at Kelly and Jamal. I could see they were as shocked and confused as I was.

"It was me," Dad said. "I moved the tank. So you can see how ridiculous your story is." He scratched his beard. "I really don't understand the three of you. But I'll be home later, and I'll be expecting your apology."

"What are you going to do now?" I asked in a tiny voice.

"Send you home, of course. I have a car outside. It will take you home. And I don't expect you to go anywhere. Wait till I get home, and we're going to have a long, long talk. You too, Jamal."

I sighed. Okay. Okay. We were wrong about the propane tank. Maybe it *was* a crazy story to begin with. But we were right about the dummies. They were alive, and they were evil. And they were plotting against Dad.

We were right and Dad was wrong.

But as we rode home in the black Town Car Dad had shoved us into, we agreed there was no way we could ever convince him of the truth.

"He'll never trust us again," Kelly said, shaking her head. She had tears in her eyes. "No matter what we tell him, he'll think of the dummy story, and he won't believe us."

"But what if we *prove* to your father that the dummies are alive?" Jamal asked.

I had my head propped up in my hands. I groaned. "How do we do that? We already tried like a million times, remember?"

Jamal nodded.

"The dummies go limp and lifeless whenever they feel like it," Kelly said. "We can't prove anything to Dad. We're sunk. Totally sunk."

We rode the rest of the way home in glum silence.

It's a terrible feeling to know your dad thinks you are a liar. I guess I don't need to say that. Everyone knows it. But as the car climbed the Hollywood Hills to our house, I had to fight back the tears. I don't think I'd ever felt worse in my life.

We passed the low wall at the front of our yard, and the car turned and began to crunch over the gravel driveway. We came to a stop at the stone walk that leads to our front door.

I leaned over the seat and thanked the driver. He had a cap over his head and I couldn't see his face. "Have a good one," he called, without turning around.

The sun still shone brightly as the three of us piled out of the back seat. The flowers swayed and shimmered in the flower beds at both sides of the walk.

I sighed again and started to slump toward the house.

"Look on the bright side," Jamal said. "At least no one is going to get blown up at your dad's studio."

I started to reply—but stopped when I heard a *clank* from the driveway. Startled, I spun around in time to see the trunk lid on the black Town Car pop open.

"Oh no!" A cry burst from my throat. Slappy and Snappy sat up.

The driver had already started to back down the driveway. But the two dummies scrambled out of the trunk. The trunk lid slammed shut as they landed on their feet on the gravel, their legs bobbing until they caught their balance.

Then they both staggered toward us as the car disappeared down the hill.

"Aren't you going to welcome us home?" Slappy shouted. He tossed back his head and laughed. *"Now it's time for a REAL horror show!"*

28

Jamal's mouth hung open. Kelly took a step back and shot her arms out as if getting ready for a fight.

"What do you want?" I cried. "Why did you follow us home?"

"We don't like you talking about us to your dad!" Slappy shouted. *"And . . . we just plain don't* like *you! Hahaha."*

Snappy swung an arm up and bumped his wooden hand against his twin's shoulder. *"Why are you such a hater, Slappy?"* he demanded. *"You have to deal with your anger issues."*

"Here's how I deal with my anger issues!" Slappy cried. He leaped forward, arms raised in front of him. And before I could move, he jumped onto my back.

"Get OFF!" I screamed.

I tried to twist and toss him away. But the dummy wrapped his arms around me and held on. "Owwww!" I cried out in pain as he bashed his wooden head into the back of my neck.

I ducked. I dropped to my knees. I spun around hard. But I couldn't throw him off.

Kelly screamed. I saw Jamal hunched beside her, frozen in horror.

Slappy head-butted me again. And slapped my face with a hard wooden fist. *"Well, well, Luke!"* he cried. *"Who's the dummy now?"*

He gave me a hard shove and I toppled face-first to the grass. My head hit the dirt. Pain shot down my body. He drove a fist into the back of my neck.

"Stop it, Slappy. You know I don't approve of violence!" Snappy shouted.

And then to my surprise, Snappy bent over us and began tugging Slappy with both hands. Tugging Slappy off me.

I felt Slappy's hands loosen and slide away. The two dummies tumbled into a heap on the lawn. I backed away, dizzy, my head still throbbing.

They untangled themselves and scrambled to their feet. Slappy gave his twin a hard shove. *"Guess what I'm going to do on the next cold night?"* he cried. *"Use your head for firewood!"*

"Now, now, Slappy," Snappy scolded. *"You know you have a temper problem."*

"My only problem is YOU—you weak piece of kindling!" Slappy screamed.

Before Snappy could react, Slappy swung his

fist and punched him in the head. The punch made a loud *clonnnk*.

Snappy staggered back, lost his balance, and fell to the grass. He let out a long groan and shook his head, dazed.

Kelly, Jamal, and I cried out as Slappy strode up to his twin and *kicked* him in the head with his heavy wooden shoe.

Snappy groaned again. He dodged another kick and scrambled to his feet. He staggered forward and wrapped his arms around Slappy's shoulders, and dragged him to the ground.

The three of us watched in shock as the dummies wrestled, rolling around, punching, head-butting, groaning, and screaming angrily.

"They're going to tear each other apart!" Jamal cried, hands pressed against his cheeks.

But then Snappy freed himself from Slappy's grip. He pulled himself up, shook his whole body hard, then started to run.

Slappy leaped to his feet. His jaw clicked up and down. And then he shouted, *"Run, you crybaby! I'll chop you into splinters!"*

He took off after his twin, shaking a fist in the air.

"Where are they going?" Kelly demanded.

We watched them run along the side of the house. "Come on," I said. I began to run after them.

"Should we call the police or something?" Jamal asked, trotting beside me.

I squinted at him. "Huh? Call the police and say what? Two dummies are fighting in our backyard?"

"They're going into the garage!" Kelly cried, pointing.

I lowered my head and ran faster. I was desperate to see how this was going to end up.

To my surprise, the dummies reached the garage but didn't go inside. Instead, they ran alongside it, heading around back.

"Oh nooo!" A high wail burst from my throat. "The propane tank. That's where it is!"

Behind the garage, Slappy caught up to Snappy and spun him around. He landed a hard punch in Snappy's belly. Snappy grabbed his twin's head in both hands and pulled. The *craaaack* of the head-butt echoed off the trees.

They fought along the garage wall. Then they stumbled into the yard behind the garage.

"The propane tank!" I shouted. "Stay away from the propane tank!"

Gasping for breath, I reached the back of the garage, turned—and saw the tall tank tilting slightly away from the garage wall.

"Stay away from it!" I screamed, my voice cracking. "Stay away!"

But the two dummies were too involved in their battle to hear me.

"Oh noooo!" I heard Kelly's long moan behind me. And I heard Jamal's wheezing breaths.

And then, without saying a word to one another, the three of us were diving behind the low hedges at the side of the yard. Ducking for cover. Hurtling ourselves behind the safety of the hedges—because we saw what was about to happen.

We saw the battling, punching dummies stagger and stumble toward the tank. Screaming and groaning, they punched and wrestled—and tumbled closer . . . closer . . .

And then all three of us cried out as Slappy picked Snappy up off the ground—and heaved him with all his might into the tank.

I shut my eyes tight. I held my breath.

Would the tank explode?

29

Yes, it did.

I heard a *bump* as the heavy tank hit the ground. Then I heard a crackling sound, like the crack of distant thunder.

And then the thunder wasn't distant. It was right overhead. Then it was all around, a deafening *boooom* that hurt my ears, shook the ground, and made the hedges in front of us tremble.

I opened my eyes in time to see a wall of flame shoot up like a tall wave over the back of the garage. I felt a powerful burst of heat against my face. Like a strong, hot wind, it pushed me back and flattened me on the ground. It swept over me with a roar, drowning out my shrieks of horror.

I raised my head in time to see the garage burst apart. The roof flew up, and the walls crumbled and fell. And as the roof sailed to the sky, spinning as it rose, I heard shrill screams.

The dummies screamed and wailed as they were blasted into the air. Their arms and legs fluttered in the explosion as if they were swimming.

One of them sailed high and far. Squinting into the hot flames, I saw him swoop over the trees, down the sloping hill. It looked like he might fly forever. He was gone in a few seconds, out of sight.

The other dummy landed with a *thud* on the grass at the back of our lawn. He bounced twice, then didn't move.

"The garage is on fire!" Kelly's scream shook me from my daze.

I could still feel the heat of the explosion on my face. I turned to Kelly and Jamal. "Are you okay?"

Kelly's cheeks were red and her hair was standing straight up on her head. Jamal kept blinking his eyes and swallowing. He pulled a jagged stick of wood from his hair.

Flames danced over the broken, crumpled ruins of the garage. Lawn tools were scattered over the grass. A wheelbarrow floated in the swimming pool. The fire crackled and spit.

"Got to call 911!" I shouted. I turned toward the house—and gasped.

There stood Dad at the edge of the driveway.

I could see the flames reflected in his dark eyes. He had the angriest expression I'd ever seen on his face.

"Dad—" I started. "You've *got* to believe us . . ."

30

He hurried over to us. "Are you all okay? You didn't get hurt?"

"We're okay," I said.

"Just a little shaken," Jamal said.

Kelly rubbed her cheek. "My face feels sunburned."

"Oh, thank goodness," Dad said. He wrapped the three of us in a hug.

Then he pulled out his phone. "Let me call 911. Get the fire department out here before the fire spreads."

I waited until he stopped talking and tucked the phone back into his pocket. Boards crackled as a section of the burning rafters collapsed.

I took a deep breath. "Dad, I know you won't believe us," I said. "But we didn't blow up the garage. The dummies—"

He raised a hand to silence me.

"No, Dad," I protested. "You've got to let us

talk. The dummies knocked over the tank and caused the explosion."

He still had his hand raised. "I know," he said.

All three of us cried out.

"What did you say?" Kelly demanded.

"I *know* the dummies did it," Dad said.

We stared at him. I let out a long sigh of relief.

"I decided to follow you home," Dad explained. "I was worried about you because of all that crazy dummy talk. I thought you three were living in some kind of fantasy world. When I got here, I saw the dummies fighting."

I gasped. "You saw them?"

Dad nodded. "So . . ." He rubbed his beard. "So I realized I'd been wrong. I'd been acting like a jerk. I should have believed you kids right from the beginning."

I heard sirens in the distance. The fire trucks were on the way.

The flames had died down a bit. Clouds of black smoke rose from the smoldering boards.

"I saw the dummies wrestling and trying to kill each other," Dad continued, speaking softly. "I was too much in shock to try and stop them. And I never *dreamed* their fight would end up blowing our garage to pieces."

"We tried to tell you—" Jamal insisted.

Dad nodded. "I know. I owe you kids a million apologies. I really do." His expression brightened.

"But don't worry. I'm going to take care of these two evil dummies—right now."

"One of them was blown away in the explosion," I said.

Dad nodded again. "I know. I saw him go. Good riddance. And now I'm going to get rid of this one, too."

He reached down and lifted the dummy off the grass.

"Dad—what are you going to do?" I asked.

"Toss him in the fire," Dad said, taking a few steps toward the crackling flames at the back wall.

"But you said the dummies are valuable," Kelly said.

Dad raised the dummy in front of him. "I don't care. They're not as valuable as believing in my kids. Say good-bye to this evil thing."

He raised the dummy above his head and started to heave it into the flames.

"No—Dad!" I cried, grabbing his arm. "Wait!"

31

Dad hesitated with the dummy raised in the air. "Luke? What's your problem?"

"One of the dummies is *good*," I explained. "The one named Snappy is the good one. He's always trying to get his brother Slappy to be nice."

"Luke is right," Kelly chimed in. "If this dummy is Snappy, Dad, you don't have to destroy him. It's Slappy who is the evil one."

Dad lowered the dummy in front of him. "Are you sure?"

"Yes, Dad. I'm sure. Really. You can believe us."

Dad turned the dummy around in his hands and studied it. "Well, how can you tell? They're identical. How can you tell one from the other?"

"It's easy," Jamal spoke up. "Slappy, the evil one, has green eyes. The good twin has black eyes."

All three of us turned to study the dummy's eyes. Black.

"This is Snappy," I told my dad. "You don't have to burn him. He's okay. He's the good one."

Dad squinted at the dummy. "Well . . ."

Fire trucks roared to a stop at the bottom of our driveway. The sirens all wailed their shrill warning, making birds fly up from all the trees. Black-uniformed firefighters in boots and long rubber slickers came leaping off the trucks.

Dad shoved Snappy into my arms and hurried to meet them. "This way, guys!" he shouted, waving wildly. "This way!"

I gazed at Snappy. The collar of his white shirt was burned brown from the fire and one jacket sleeve had a ragged black burn at the cuff. Otherwise, he seemed untouched by the flames.

I carried him up to Dad's horror museum in the attic and sat him down on the top of the glass display case. The three of us stood watching him.

"Snappy," I said. "Are you still alive? Can you hear us?"

His jaw clicked noisily up and down. His black eyes blinked.

"Thanks for rescuing me," he said. *"Now I don't have to pretend to be nice anymore."*

I swallowed. "Pretend?"

He nodded. *"Slappy thought it was fun for me to fool you. But do you have any idea how hard it was for me to be the good one? But he's gone now, and I'm here . . . and it's no more Mr. Nice Guy. Line up, slaves! Stand at attention when your new master speaks to you!"*

"But—but—Snappy—" I stammered.

"Let's start our new movie!" he cried. *"What shall we call it? How about SNAPPY RULES!"*

EPILOGUE

Wow, dudes. That ending was a BLAST—wasn't it?

I was sorry to fly off without saying good-bye. No one even wished me "Happy landings!" Hahaha!

At least those kids got their drone to fly. Too bad the rest of the garage had to fly *with* it! Haha.

Well . . . don't worry about me, slaves. I don't go to pieces when these little accidents happen. I'll get myself together real soon.

Don't think you can escape Slappy. I'll be back before you know it with another Goosebumps story.

Remember, this is *SlappyWorld*.

You only *scream* in it!

PLEASE DO NOT FEED THE WEIRDO

Here's a sneak peek!

I took a big bite of the fluffy blue candy. I could feel the powdery sugar stick to my face.

Karla pointed to the cone in my hand. "Jordan, you have a spider in your cotton candy," she said.

I let out a loud "ULLLLLLP!" and the cone went flying into the air. I watched it land with a soft *plop* onto the pavement.

Karla tossed back her head and laughed. "You're too easy!"

Mom shook her head. "Karla, why are you always scaring your brother?"

She grinned. "Because it's fun?"

Grumbling to myself, I bent down and picked the cotton candy off the ground. Some of the blue stuff stuck to my sneakers. I took another bite anyway.

Some kids like to be scared and some don't. And I totally don't. I saw the Tunnel of Fear up ahead, and I knew Karla would force me to go in there with her.

My name is Jordan Keppler, and I'm twelve, a year older than Karla. I don't like to brag, but . . . I get better grades than Karla, and I'm better at sports than Karla, and I have more friends than Karla does.

So just because she likes scary things and I don't doesn't make her any kind of big deal.

I looked all around. Carnival World was crowded because it was a beautiful spring night. I saw dozens of kids on the boardwalk, going from the game booths to the rides. And I knew a lot of them were walking right past the Tunnel of Fear because they were like me.

What's the fun of screaming your head off anyway?

I tossed my cotton candy cone in a trash can. "Where's that ride with the swings that go really high?" I asked.

"You mean that baby ride in the kiddie park?" Karla said.

Dad leaned over and took a big bite of Karla's cotton candy. "If you two want to go into the Tunnel of Fear, Mom and I will wait here," he said.

"No, thanks," I said. "I'll wait out here, too."

Karla pressed her hands against her waist and tossed back her curly red hair. "Well, I'm not going in alone, jerkface."

"Don't call your brother names," Mom said.

"I didn't," Karla replied. "That is his name." She thinks she's so smart and funny.

"Don't make your sister go in there alone," Dad said. He put his hands on my shoulders. "Jordan, you're not scared, are you?"

He *knew* I was scared. Why bother to ask?

"Of *course* I'm not scared," I said. "It's just that . . . I ate all that cotton candy. I have to sit down and digest it."

I know. I know. That was lame. You don't have to tell me.

Karla grabbed my hand and tugged me hard toward the entrance. "Come on, Jordan. They only bring us to the carnival once a year. We have to do *everything*."

I turned back to Mom and Dad. They were both making shooing motions with their hands. They were no help at all.

Don't get me wrong. I love Carnival World. I love the dart games and the corn dogs on a stick and the Ferris wheel and the Dunk-the-Clown water tank.

There are only two things I don't love. The rollercoaster rides that make you go upside down. And the Tunnel of Fear. And somehow— thanks to my sister—I knew I had both of those in my *near* future.

Karla and I walked up the wooden ramp to the Tunnel entrance. "See you later!" I heard Mom shout. "If you survive!"

Ha. She and Karla have the same sick sense of humor.

Purple and red lights flashed all around us, and I heard deep, evil laughter—horror-movie laughter—echoing inside the Tunnel. And screams. Lots of shrill screams. I couldn't tell if they were recorded or if they were from real people inside the ride.

Karla gave the young guy at the entrance two tickets, and he motioned us to the open cars that were moving slowly toward the dark cave opening, where the ride began.

She pushed me into a car and slid in beside me. "This is so cool," she gushed. "We should have brought a barf bag for you."

Ha again.

"It's all fake," I said. "It's all babyish scares. Too phony to be scary. Seriously."

Wish I had been right about that.

As we rolled into total blackness, the door on our moving car slammed shut. A safety bar dropped down over our legs.

The car spun quickly, then slid along an invisible track beneath us. I gripped the safety bar with both hands. My eyes squinted into the darkness. I couldn't see a thing—Until a grinning skull shot down from above. It stopped an inch from my face, and its jagged, broken teeth snapped up and down as shrill laughter floated out.

I gasped. I didn't scream. I gripped the safety bar a little tighter.

Something damp and sticky brushed my face. I raised both hands to swipe at it, to try to push it off me.

Beside me, Karla laughed. "Yucky cobwebs," she said. She poked me. "And you know if there are cobwebs, there has to be . . ."

She didn't need to say it. At least a dozen spindly, rubbery, fat black spiders bounced over the car. I tried to brush them off my face, but there were too many of them.

The car spun again, and I stared into a wall of darkness. Were there other people in the tunnel? I couldn't see them and I couldn't hear them.

Karla screamed as a huge, caped vampire figure jumped into our car. "*I want to drink your bloooood!*" it exclaimed. The vampire lowered its fangs to Karla's neck—but then disappeared.

Karla shuddered. She grabbed my sleeve. "That was creepy."

"It's all computer graphics," I said. I was trying to be the brave one. But to be honest, my stomach was doing cartwheels and my throat was suddenly as dry as cotton candy.

Then evil cackling surrounded our car, and we jolted to a stop. I rocked against the safety bar, then bounced back.

The cackling stopped.

Silence.

And then a high-pitched scream. A girl's scream that echoed off the tunnel walls.

We sat in solid darkness. My heart started to pound.

"Think there's something wrong?" Karla spoke in a whisper. For once, she was scared, too.

"We definitely stalled," I said. My hands were cold and sweaty on the safety bar. "Unless maybe this is all part of the ride. You know. An extra thrill part."

I couldn't see Karla's expression. It was too dark to see her, even though she was inches away. But I heard her rapid breaths. She squeezed my sleeve again. "It'll probably start right back up, right?"

"For sure," I said.

So we waited. Waited and listened. Listened to the heavy silence.

No voices or music or sounds from the carnival on the other side of the walls. The only thing I could hear was the throb of blood pulsing in my ears.

We waited some more.

"Cold in here," Karla murmured. "Like a tomb." She hugged herself.

"You don't think that girl's scream was a real scream—do you?" I asked. My skin still prickled.

"Why doesn't the ride start up again?" Karla said softly, ignoring my question.

"Why are we whispering?" I asked.

Even our whispers echoed in the black tunnel.

I spread my hand over my chest. I could feel my fluttering heartbeats. I had tried to be brave. But . . . I knew I was about to lose it.

I could feel a scream forming in my throat.

Feel all my muscles tighten. Feel the panic creeping up from my stomach . . . How long had we been waiting in the cold, silent darkness? Ten minutes? Fifteen? More?

I gripped the safety bar so hard my hands ached. "Hey!" The shout burst from my open mouth. "Is anyone *else* in here? Can anyone hear me? Hey!"

No answer. No one. No one else trapped in this solid blackness.

"Can anyone hear me?" I shouted again, my voice high and shrill. "Who is in here with us? Anyone here?"

Silence.

"Hey! We need help—" I couldn't finish my cry. Fingers wrapped around my neck from behind. Cold, bone-hard fingers . . . tightening. Choking me.

I twisted my head free and spun around in the car.

A grinning skeleton stared at me with its empty black eye sockets an inch from my face. Its jaw squeaked up and down—and it flew up to the darkness of the ceiling.

The icy touch of its fingers still stung my skin. I was gasping for breath now.

Karla pushed my shoulder. "What is your problem? Are you having a panic attack?"

"Didn't you see that skeleton?" I cried hoarsely. "It . . . it squeezed my neck." I raised a hand and tried to rub the cold feeling away.

Karla laughed. "You idiot. That was part of the ride."

"I don't think so," I said. "Do you notice we still aren't moving? And none of the sound effects have started up again?"

"Then what is your idea?" she demanded. "You think there's a living skeleton loose in the tunnel?"

"*Please* don't say that," I said.

She slumped back in the seat. We waited some more. I kept twisting around. I didn't want anyone to sneak up on me again.

"Doesn't anyone work in here?" I asked, my voice trembling.

We both waited some more. The air seemed to grow colder. I clamped my mouth shut when I realized my teeth were chattering.

After a few more minutes, Karla and I both started shouting.

"Can anyone hear us?"

"Get us out of here!"

"Hey—anyone?!"

"Helllllllp!"

Silence. I settled back with a long sigh.

Karla grabbed the safety bar and began to shake it. After a few tries, it popped open and slid off our legs. She started to stand up.

"What are you *doing*?" I cried.

"We have to get out of the car and walk to the exit," she said. She lowered one foot over the side.

I grabbed her and pulled her back. "No. Wait. It's . . . it's too dark."

She twisted herself free. "We can't just sit here shouting," she said. "Mom and Dad are probably worried."

"I'm worried, too," I said, my eyes darting all around. "Where's the exit? I don't see it."

"We'll just follow the tracks," Karla said. "You know. They have to lead us out."

She lowered her feet to the ground. Then she turned and tugged my arm. "Come on, Chickenface. Follow me."

"Don't call names," I said.

"I didn't."

I stayed in the seat. I didn't want to step out of the car. I guess I felt safer sitting there. But I finally forced my legs to move and climbed down beside Karla.

She began walking along the car track. I kept glancing back, making sure nothing was sneaking up on us. It was blacker than night in the tunnel. I honestly couldn't tell if my eyes were open or closed.

"Hey, wait up!" I called, my voice choked, muffled in the cold air. I squinted hard. I couldn't see Karla. "Wait up. I'm serious. You're walking too fast."

"I'm right here," she called from somewhere up ahead.

And then I stumbled. I tripped over something and fell forward.

I landed on something soft. Pain shot up my knees. I raised myself and squinted into the darkness to see what I had tripped over.

"Oh nooo," I gasped.

It was a boy. A dead boy.

I scrambled to climb off him. My hand slipped on his head. His hard wooden head.

Wait. Whoa. Not a boy. Some kind of dummy. A mannequin. Dressed in boy's clothes.

Squinting over the floor, I saw another boy mannequin. Two girl mannequins. All facedown, sprawled on the tunnel floor.

Just another scary part of the ride?

I let go of the mannequin head and pushed myself up. I'd landed hard on my right knee. I rubbed it, trying to sooth the pain away.

I stepped closer to the track and began to follow it through the darkness. I kept my eyes down. I didn't want to trip over any more mannequins.

I stopped with a gasp when I heard laughter. Cold, cruel laughter. Evil laughter in a deep woman's voice.

"Hey!" I called out. "Who's there? Is someone there?"

The creepy laughter echoed off the tunnel walls till it seemed to come from all directions.

"Karla? Is that you?" My voice came out high and shrill. "Karla?" Was she hiding or something? Playing a mean trick on me?

"Hey, Karla. Shout, okay? So I can find you? Karla?"

The cold woman's laughter seemed to come from right behind me. I spun around. Nothing but darkness.

"Karla? Come on. Are you trying to scare me? Stop it!" I shouted. "This isn't funny. Karla— where *are* you?"

I spun all around. I saw only a blur of black.

A loud *clank* made me jump. I heard an electronic hum. Another *clank*. The cars started moving again, slowly, creaking into motion.

"Karla? Hey, Karla?" I shouted over the hum and squeak of the cars.

The woman's cold laughter rang in my ears.

I gazed around again. No Karla. No Karla.

I started toward one of the slow-moving cars. And once again, an icy hand gripped the back of my neck.

About the Author

R.L. Stine's books are read all over the world. So far, his books have sold more than 300 million copies, making him one of the most popular children's authors in history. Besides Goosebumps, R.L. Stine has written the teen series Fear Street and the funny series Rotten School, as well as the Mostly Ghostly series, The Nightmare Room series, and the two-book thriller *Dangerous Girls*. R.L. Stine lives in New York with his wife, Jane, and Minnie, his King Charles spaniel. You can learn more about him at www.RLStine.com.